Zakiya's Enduring Wounds

ROOSEVELT HIGH SCHOOL SERIES

Gloria L. Velásquez

T0284387

PIÑATA
BOOKS

PIÑATA BOOKS
ARTE PÚBLICO PRESS
HOUSTON, TEXAS

Piñata Books are full of surprises!

Piñata Books
An imprint of
Arte Público Press
University of Houston
4902 Gulf Fwy, Bldg 19, Rm 100
Houston, Texas 77204-2004

Cover art by Anne Vega
Cover design by Robert Vega

Library of Congress Control Number: 202293435

♾ The paper used in this publication meets the requirements of the American National Standard for Information Sciences—Permanence of Paper for Printed Library Materials, ANSI Z39.48-1984.

Printed in the United States of America
Versa Press, Inc.,
May 2022-September 2022
5 4 3 2 1

In memory of our beloved friend
and spiritual advisor,
Rev. Father Kenneth Brown, VP
1949-2016

ONE
Zakiya

"Thanks for the ride, Mrs. Martin," I say as I slam the car door shut.

"No problem, Zakiya, you and Peyton played great today."

Waving back to Peyton and her mom as they drive away, I hurry across the street to our apartment. The moment I open the door, I can smell Momma's fried chicken. Setting my gym bag down, I glance at Jerome sitting on the floor playing his obnoxious video games. "Is Dad home?" I ask, only he's so involved in his game that he ignores my question. I'm about to yell at him when Momma pokes her head out of the kitchen.

"Did you win this time?" she asks, sounding critical like always. I don't know why Momma can't be sweet like Dad. He never acts pissy with me about anything, but not Momma, all she seems to do is complain. And she doesn't even know the slightest thing about volleyball.

"We lost, but we won two out of three in the tournament."

Just then, Dad walks into the living room. "How's my Zee baby today?" he asks, moving closer so I can give him a hug and a kiss. Ever since I can remember, Dad's called me his Zee baby and the nickname has stuck. Jerome's constantly making snide remarks about me being Daddy's little girl. I guess maybe he's right after all.

Hanging his jacket in the closet, Dad orders Jerome to turn off the TV. Jerome is about to complain, but the scowl on Dad's face makes him hesitate, so instead he disappears to his room.

"Zakiya, time to set the table," Momma hollers from the kitchen.

I stare helplessly at Dad. "I have to take a shower," I plead with him. "I smell really bad."

Sniffing several times, Dad says, "You go on—I'll take care of it."

"Thanks, Dad." I smile, pick up my gym bag and head for the stairs.

In my bedroom, I search through my dresser for a pair of warm jogging pants and a matching T-shirt. Then I go into the small bathroom that I share with Jerome and my older brother, Tyrone. It's always cluttered and messy. Tyrone leaves all his shaving stuff scattered on the counter, but the worst part is that I have to remind Jerome about a hundred times a week to put the toilet seat down. I can hardly wait until we have our own house. Maybe then we'll have two bathrooms. Dad and Momma have been saving money for years. Dad heard about this program in Laguna where they help low income families build their own homes. It's always been Momma's dream to have our own backyard where she can plant a garden with flowers and vegetables. Dad's always bringing her flowers from Discount Foods. He likes to tease Momma that she's his queen. One day I'll marry a man just like my dad.

Once I've showered and dressed, I stare at my reflection in the mirror. I wonder why I had to look like Momma with my big round eyes and fat cheekbones. The only thing I really like is my nose. It's not too big or too small. Somebody once told me it was perfectly shaped. Dad's always telling Momma she's the most beautiful woman in the world. He says I look just like her, so maybe I'm not so bad after all. If only I weren't so tall. I'm the tallest girl on the volleyball team, which is a good thing, still it seems like a lot of guys go for girls who are shorter. But Peyton insists I have nothing to worry because I have "long, sexy legs."

By the time I come back downstairs for dinner, everyone is already seated at the kitchen table, even Tyrone. Sometimes he can't make it for dinner because of a class, but Momma makes sure to save him a plate of food. It's Tyrone's first year at Laguna University. He's working on a Social Sciences degree so he can become a counselor. Ever since Tyrone worked at the Teen Center, he says he wants to be like Mr. G. and help others.

"Sure took you a long time," Jerome complains, as I sit next to Tyrone. His plate is piled high with mashed potatoes and gravy. I'll never understand how he can eat that much and stay so thin. Guess he took after Dad and I took after Momma, big and bulky.

While I serve myself two pieces of fried chicken, I ask Tyrone, "How are your classes—any cute guys?"

Ignoring my question, Tyrone describes the project they're working on in one of his classes. From the corner of my eye, I can see Momma's face light up. Tyrone will be the first one in our family to graduate from a university. Dad graduated from high school while Momma only went to eighth grade. One time I heard Dad bragging to one of his customers about how Tyrone was going to be a real professional and not work in a grocery store like him.

"What about you?" Tyrone asks, serving himself a second helping of mashed potatoes and gravy. "What's up at ol' Roosevelt?"

"Everything's cool. I'm gonna join the dance troupe next semester."

"With that clunky body?" Jerome asks. The facetious grin on his face makes me want to slap him.

Dad quickly comes to my defense, telling Jerome to mind his own business. I'll never understand why I have to have a snotty twelve-year-old brother like him. Why can't he act more like Tyrone? Tyrone's always been kind and considerate, but not Jerome. He's a punk, always making fun of me and my friends.

Shoving the last bit of mashed potatoes in his mouth, Tyrone pushes back his chair. "Sorry, Momma," he apologizes. "I have to attend a lecture this evening—have to run now."

"Better hurry, son," Dad tells him as he bends down to give Momma a kiss on the cheek.

"You go on now. We'll take care of the dishes," Momma tells him as he exits the kitchen.

Momma's constantly catering to Tyrone and Jerome, but I know if it were me who had to rush out, she wouldn't act the same way. Peyton said her mom's also like that with her older brother, that she babies and treats him like he's a king.

When we're done eating, Dad orders Jerome to help me with the dishes while he and Momma go into the living room to watch TV. Dad always massages Momma's feet while they watch the evening news, you'd think they were newlyweds, the way Dad gushes over Momma. But I guess that's better than arguing. Peyton says her parents have heated fights and one time her dad even moved out for a month. I've never told her about how Dad left Momma when his drinking got bad. But he came back home and has been going to A.A. since then. There're so many students at school whose parents are divorced and I'm just grateful to have both parents. I wouldn't trade them for a million bucks.

I can tell Jerome is pissed about having to dry the dishes for Tyrone because he splashes water all over the counter. I'm about to get started on the pots and pans, when Jerome flings the dishtowel on the counter.

"I'm out of here—I have tons of homework."

"Liar!" I call out, as he hurries out the kitchen. I know he just wants to go upstairs to watch stupid skater videos. *But what do I care, anyway?* I can get the dishes done faster without him.

I'm reaching for Momma's favorite wrought-iron skillet, when Dad walks back into the kitchen. "Need some help?" he asks, picking up a clean dishcloth.

"Thanks, Dad. That lazy Jerome quit on me."

"That's what I figured—so how's volleyball? I hope it isn't taking too much time from your homework?"

Dipping the silverware into the soapy water, I smile up at him. "No, it's not. I can get a lot done during study hall."

"That's real fine because I want you to get into the university like your brother did. Be somebody."

"Well, I'm gonna be a dancer," I say, drying my hands quickly. "Wanna see one of my dance moves?"

Before he can reply, I start to do one of my dance routines, my hands swaying to the rhythm of my body. Smiling, Dad begins to clap just as Momma comes walking into the kitchen.

"What's all the commotion here?" she asks in a loud, obnoxious voice.

"Zee baby thinks she knows how to dance, but she doesn't know nothing."

The next thing I know Dad pulls Momma into his arms and they start to waltz around the kitchen as if they were in a huge ballroom. Momma's face is flushed by the time they come to a halt. His handsome face beaming with pride, Dad confesses, "There was a time when your momma and I used to be the best ones on the dance floor."

"Those were some good days, weren't they, Jerry?" Momma grins and says, "Now, why don't I help Zakiya finish up here?"

"Margaret, you mind your own business," Dad says, insisting Momma go back into the living room.

Dipping my hands back into the soapy water, I ask gently, "Dad, why didn't you go to college?"

"I wanted to," he admits, his voice low and soft. "But there never seemed to be enough money. Seems like my daddy was always struggling to put food on the table."

"What about Momma?"

"Her parents were poor too, and she had to help take care of her younger brothers and sisters. Your momma was the smart one. When I met her, all she did was read. She loved poetry—Langston Hughes was her favorite. Then after we got married and the babies started coming . . . it was just too hard for her to go to school. But you and Tyrone are gonna make us both very proud."

I dry my hands as fast as I can and reach out to embrace him. "I'm the one who's proud of *you*, Dad," I whisper "You're the best father in the world."

TWO
Zakiya

As the bus pulls up to the stop, I think back to how freaked out I was last year. It was my freshman year at Roosevelt and I wondered how I was going to find my way around such a huge campus. It's a good thing I had a nice friend like Dalana so that I wouldn't feel like I was the only black girl around. This year I love being a sophomore, feeling big and bad compared to those wimpy freshman. I've made lots of new friends on the volleyball team like Peyton. And even though she's white, we have a lot in common. We both have older brothers and we both like hip-hop. Though I have to admit, it was a little weird the first time I went to Peyton's house, the way her parents stared at me. I've often heard Mom and Dad talking about how different white people are, but Peyton's parents turned out to be super nice, after they stopped staring.

Peyton is waiting for me near the steps to the main quad like she does almost every morning. "Don't look, but Carlos is checking you out again," she says, her small blue eyes glittering.

Out of the corner of my eye, I spot Carlos standing by the Science building talking to another guy. He is definitely staring at me. My heart does several flip flops. Carlos is in my Spanish class and he just moved here from the Bay area. He is such a hunk with his wavy, black hair and the most gorgeous green eyes I've ever seen.

As we head for our lockers, I tease Peyton, "Are you sure he's not checking *you* out?" If anyone is always checking guys out, it's her. That's all she ever talks about. Not that I don't check out guys myself, but she seems obsessed with having a boyfriend. Peyton's short and skinny—she's always telling me I'm lucky 'cause guys go for girls with good-sized boobs like mine.

My first class of the day is English, which I really like because this semester we're reading poetry. Mrs. Harrison doesn't get carried away with analyzing rhyme or technique. She likes to focus on the message of the poem and how it relates to what is happening in society today. Another thing I really like about her teaching is that we don't just read the famous white poets like that Whitman guy. Last week we read Maya Angelou's poetry and next week we're reading Ntozake Shange—I've never even heard of her.

As soon as second period ends, I rush out the door for my favorite class of the day—performing arts. It's way over in the gym and it takes me a while to get there, only I could care less. I love to dance and I love any kind of movement. Momma always complains that when I was a little girl, she could never keep me still for very long. But Dad's eyes light up as he tells stories about how I would dance around the room like a swan any time music was playing.

By the time I've changed into my black yoga pants, Dalana has saved a spot for me on the gym floor. We've been best friends since junior high, so we always sit together. Today Mrs. Jessup spends the entire period lecturing on technique. When a girl raises her hand to ask why we have to warm-up before we begin to dance, she talks about body placement and alignment. She emphasizes that without the correct warm-ups we can hurt our muscles. Dalana giggles when I tell her, "I'd like to hurt Jerome, give him a smack sometime, he's a pain in the ass."

After Biology, I hurry to meet Peyton at the snack cart. Then we find a quiet spot over by the multi-purpose room where we can eat our lunch in peace. Sometimes Dalana joins us, but lately it seems like she's always got some kind of project for her robotics class. It's either that or she's having lunch with Moses. They've become really good friends since they realized they have fathers who are in prison. Dalana always sounds so cheerful when she talks about visiting her dad at the prison. As for me, I can't ever imagine not having my dad around. I mean, I can because we went through it when he was drinking a lot, but he came back. Dalana's dad isn't coming home anytime soon.

As I bite into my ham sandwich, Peyton reaches for her phone to show me her new love interest. "His name is Tanner. He's so hot—he's a senior at San Martin High."

"He's cute," I agree, noticing his black and white letterman jacket.

"He's on the football team."

"Cool," I tell her.

Slipping her phone back into her pocket, Peyton says, "No volleyball today. Want to go downtown?"

"I better not since I didn't let Momma know." Peyton and I love to go downtown to all the stores. Laguna has the most expensive clothing stores in the area. Peyton and I will spend hours checking out cute tops and jeans. Sometimes we try clothes on just for the heck of it even though we don't have any money to buy anything.

"How about a ride home, then?" she asks. "I can text Alan to pick us up."

"Cool—then I won't have to ride that stupid bus." Alan is Peyton's brother and a senior this year. Peyton will often coax him into giving us a ride home after school. I remember the first time Alan dropped me off at my apartment. I felt slightly embarrassed because they live in a big house in an upscale neighborhood. But I didn't let it get to me. Besides, I love my family. And like Dad's always saying, one day he's gonna buy Momma her dream house.

My last period of the day is beginner Spanish. I really like the teacher, Mr. Villamil, but I'm always on edge since Carlos is in that class. When Mr. Villamil instructs us to pair up and practice the textbook exercises with the verb "gustar," Carlos is suddenly at my side. "Let me hear your *español*." He smiles, taking the empty chair next to me.

My palms feel sweaty and my heart is beating fast like a conga drum. "This must be easy for you," I stammer.

"Yeah, it's fun." His green eyes draw me in like a magnet.

"Do you speak Spanish at home?"

Shaking his head, Carlos says, "Mostly with my grandparents, who are from Mexico. I can speak it, but I never learned to write it, that's why I'm in this class. Ever since I was little my grandma used to always speak Spanish to us. I'm kind of glad she did."

"That's nice," I tell him.

Just then, Mr. Villamil, who is now circulating the room, pauses at our side. Carlos focuses his eyes on the exercises. "*¿Te gusta bailar?*" he asks.

"*Sí, yo me gusto bailar*," I answer, and Mr. Villamil takes a moment to correct me.

As soon as he's out of distance, Carlos switches back to English, "I hear you're a very good dancer."

"I love to dance," I reply, feeling excited to find out he's been asking about me. I wonder if Peyton's right, that he does like me. All I know is he's the hottest guy on campus.

"Do you dance any *cumbias*?" he asks with a sly grin.

"What's that?"

A huge smile spreads across Carlos' brown face and I wonder if I've said something stupid. When Mr. Villamil signals for everyone to return to their seats, I do my best not to stare as Carlos stands up, wishing we could talk more.

After school, Peyton and I sit on the steps near the bus stop to wait for Alan. When Peyton puts on a music video, I stand up and begin to sway back and forth to the rhythm. Shaking her head, Peyton sighs, "If only I could dance like you."

"Come on, I'll show you," I say, grabbing her hand just as Alan pulls up to the curb in his red Honda.

"You're late," Peyton scolds Alan as we both climb into the car.

Alan apologizes, "Sorry, we had a meeting about our senior project." Glancing toward the back seat, he says, "Hey, Zakiya, some hot dance moves there."

Thanking him, I smile to myself, remembering how Alan's always saying that white people don't have any rhythm. As he drives out of the parking lot, I lean forward to ask, "Would you mind dropping me off at Discount Foods? I think I'll surprise Dad."

"Sure thing," Alan says while Peyton turns up the radio, drowning out his voice.

When they drop me off at Discount Foods, I head straight toward the back, waving at Maureen, the red-headed checker who has been Dad's friend since I was in junior high. The second Dad sees me, he comes out from behind the seafood counter where he's just finished waiting on a customer. With a look of surprise on his face, he asks, "Zee baby, what are you doing here?"

"No volleyball today so Peyton's brother gave us a ride. Thought I'd surprise you."

Last month Dad was promoted to Seafood Manager. I've never seen Momma so excited. She made Dad this huge dinner with gumbo, red beans and rice. All they talked about was how much sooner they'd be able to save up for a house. I swear there were tears in Dad's eyes when Momma made us raise our water glasses to make a toast. Jerome almost ruined it when he made an idiotic wisecrack about wishing it were wine. Ever since Dad's been in A.A., that's something we should never joke about in the house.

Once Dad has clocked out, he puts on his jacket and we make our way to the front of the store. Maureen, who has a long line of customers, manages to holler out, "So they're checking up on you, Jerry?"

His lips parting, Dad waves back. "Wouldn't have it any other way."

On the drive home, Dad asks me loads of questions about my classes. When I tell him I got an A on my poetry essay, his face lights up. "Zee, you're not just pretty like your momma, but you're smart too!"

"Thanks, Dad." I smile back, asking him if I can turn the radio on, knowing that he always lets me have my way. When hip-hop comes on, Dad sticks his left arm up in the air as if he's dancing. We both start to giggle as we dance in our seats all the way back to the apartment. I suddenly find myself wishing we lived hours away so I could spend more time alone with him, so I could have him all to myself before Momma commands all his attention.

THREE
Zakiya

It's Wednesday morning and I've just walked into my Algebra class when my name is called over the intercom.

"Saved by the bell," Mr. B says, handing me a pass. "We'll be reviewing last night's assignment."

Trying to act as if I care, I thank him and go back out to the hallway. If Mr. B only knew how happy I am to get out of Math even for a few minutes.

Though the sky is grey and it smells like it might rain, I take my sweet time walking to the main quad. As I pause to try a dance move I saw on YouTube last night, I wonder if it's my counselor who wants to see me. I still haven't finished registering for my classes for my junior year. That's gotta be it.

My eyes nearly pop out of my head when I walk into the main office to find Tyrone slumped down in a chair. He raises his head, then stands up. His eyes are bloodshot as if he hasn't slept all night.

"Zee, you have to come home now," he explains. "I already checked you out."

"What's up?" I ask, a shiver running down my spine. The last time I saw that frantic look on his face was when

Dad took off and Tyrone had to drop out of school to help Momma pay the bills. Taking me by the hand, he leads me gently out the door while Mrs. Leigh pretends to busy herself with paperwork.

"But I still have one more period," I argue, as we head out of the building.

His voice barely a whisper, Tyrone says, "Dad had a heart attack."

Frozen in my steps, I say, "You're joking, right?"

Tyrone shakes his head, placing his arm around my shoulder as I burst into tears. Pulling my head against his chest, he strokes my hair gently. After a minute or two, he takes me by the hand again and leads me toward the parking lot. By the time we reach Tyrone's car, I feel completely numb as if I'm in the midst of a black hole. I let Tyrone open the door for me, but the sight of Jerome sitting in the front seat with his headphones on listening to music, makes me explode.

"What's the matter with you?" I angrily shout as I climb into the back seat. Tyrone quietly reaches over and yanks the cell phone out of Jerome's hand.

Leaning back against the car seat, I cry silently as Tyrone drives out of the parking lot and onto the busy streets. After a very long silence, Tyrone raises his voice to say, "Momma said that when Dad got up this morning for work, he felt sick to his stomach, so she insisted he stay home. But you know how stubborn Dad is, he said they needed him at work." Tyrone's voice cracks and he pauses for a few seconds to clear his voice. "One of the meat clerks found him on the floor. They rushed him to the Emergency Room but it was too late."

"Can't you just shut up?" Jerome says, leaning his head against the car window.

Knives are piercing every inch of my body and I'm suddenly drowning in rivers of blood. Closing my eyes, I curl up sideways on the seat. How could God let this happen? Why did it have to be my dad? He wasn't even fifty years old. Now he'll never be able to buy Momma a house. To take me to my high school graduation.

When we pull up to our building, Tyrone tries to help me out of the car, only I push away his hand. Jerome mumbles something about going to the basketball court as we cross the street in silence toward our apartment.

Mrs. Caldwell, one of Momma's church friends, opens the door for us. While she offers her condolences, Father Brown, our church's priest, rises from the couch. Father Brown and Dad became close friends when they found out both of them had grandparents who were from the same neighborhood in New Orleans. I always thought it was a little weird to have a priest as a best friend, but Dad used to joke that it was his way of ensuring he'd walk through those pearly gates.

"Your mother is in her room," Father Brown explains, a solemn look on his face. "The doctor gave her a sedative." Squeezing Tyrone's shoulder, he tells both of us, "I'm very sorry, but your dad is with God now."

I'm about to blurt out that I don't believe in God anymore, but I remember how much Dad respected Father Brown, so instead I nod quietly. I disappear to my bedroom, locking the door behind me.

I spend the entire day in bed, my head buried in the pillow, sobbing fiercely. I can hear people coming and going, but I refuse to go back downstairs. Later that night, there is a persistent knocking on the door. I holler out for them to go away, only it's Aunt Marilyn, Dad's sister who lives in the Bay Area. Aunt Marilyn's always been my favorite aunt because she shares my love of music and dancing so I rise slowly. It's hard to peel my body from the bed but I get up and unlock the door.

"Honey, you have to eat something," Aunt Marilyn says, as I go back to my wet pillow.

Setting the plate of food that she's carrying on top of my dresser, she comes over to sit on the edge of the bed.

"I'm not hungry," I whisper, noticing that her eyelids are puffy and it's the first time I've seen her without any make-up.

The next thing I know, Aunt Marilyn reaches down to wrap her arms around me and soon we're both crying.

∾ ∾ ∾

For the next few days, friends and neighbors fill our apartment, offering their condolences to Momma. Tyrone and I force ourselves to go downstairs for brief moments while Jerome takes off with his friends. It's no surprise that so many people come by to pay their respects. Dad was the friendliest man in the world. Whenever any of the neighbors needed help, they came looking for him, like the time Mrs. Pantoja's car wouldn't start or when Mr. Ortega got sick and didn't have enough money to pay his rent. Even some of Dad's co-workers from Discount Foods come by like Maureen, who breaks down completely in Momma's arms.

I'm not exactly sure what to do when Dalana and Peyton show up on Friday, so I invite them to the playground so we can have some privacy. The playground is empty except for a couple of bleary-eyed mothers pushing their toddlers on the baby swings. My chest tightens as I remember how Dad would take us to the playground whenever Momma left him to babysit us. He would push us high up on the swings with his thick hands that always smelled like pine because of his favorite soap.

"Hey," Dalana says, bringing me back to the present moment. "I heard a new song this morning that you might like."

"Oh, yeah," I say, pretending to be interested. The last thing I want to do is think about music.

Peyton reaches out to touch my hand. "Yeah, I'll show it to you later. Anyway, Carlos was asking about you."

When I shrug my shoulders, she refuses to give up. "We missed you at volleyball. We lost the last game and I know it's because you weren't there."

Glaring at Peyton, I can feel my face burning. "Who gives a shit about volleyball, about music? Why can't you both just leave me alone?!" I take off running back to the apartment.

∽ ∽ ∽

The day of the funeral is a total blur, like one of those Dalí paintings: distorted, surreal, images all jumbled together. I don't even remember getting dressed. Not even Momma's sobs seem to disrupt the trance I'm in as I climb into the black limousine with her and my brothers. Later, sitting in the front pew at St. Patrick's next to Aunt Marilyn and Uncle Ted, I don't hear a single word of Father Brown's sermon. I'm too broken up inside to hear anyone or anything.

At the cemetery, we gather around to watch as they lower Dad's casket into the ground. Momma's cries grow louder as she and Aunt Marilyn cling to each other. Jerome is detached like always, but I can feel the weight of Tyrone's grief suffocating me. It's almost as if I died, like I'm the one with earth being poured over her.

After the funeral, we return to the apartment where Mrs. Pantoja and several other neighbors have prepared food for everyone. The apartment fills up with lots of people again, only now it seems like it's some kind of celebration or party. Aunt Marilyn shares story after story about Dad when they were teenagers, like the time he caught her making out with a guy and Dad ran him off.

Smiling, Maureen joins in, "I can imagine Jerry doing just that. One time he scared the daylights out of this customer who was being extremely rude to me."

Momma remains quiet. She's in and out of the kitchen making sure everyone has enough to eat, but I can see the emptiness in her face and hear it in her words. For once, I pity Momma, I know how much she and Dad loved each other.

While everyone is busy eating, Tyrone comes over to my side and whispers, "Come on, let's go for a drive."

We carefully sneak out the front door to Tyrone's car. We drive around the neighborhood in silence until Tyrone finally parks at the lake.

"You know, Zee," he says, turning to me. "You've still got me."

As I gaze into his tender eyes, I can't help but remember how anytime Dad took Momma out somewhere, he always made sure to remind us that Tyrone was the man of the house. I burst into tears and Tyrone slides closer to me, putting his arm around me. And it is as if Dad were the one holding me tight.

FOUR
Dr. Martínez

The moment I opened the door, Sonia waved at me from the back of the small, cozy restaurant where she was seated at a corner table. The Thai-Na-Mite had quickly become one of our favorite places to meet since it was near Laguna University and Sonia could easily hurry back to teach her next class.

"Hope you're hungry," Sonia said, tucking a strand of dark, brown hair behind her ears. "I already ordered for us." She was dressed in a sleek blue blazer with black linen ankle pants. As one of the few professors of color at Laguna University, Sonia was a familiar voice on campus speaking out for underrepresented students.

"You're looking very professorial today," I said, pulling out the empty chair across from her.

"Blame it on the faculty meeting." She winced. "How's it been going at the office?"

It had only been a few months since I'd returned to my private practice and started seeing clients again. Avoiding Sonia's stare, I wondered if I should lie, say everything was fine, but Sonia could always see right through me. After all, we'd been *comadres* all these years, confiding in each

other, helping each other survive some rough times—
divorce, illness, intense issues that affected our youth.

"Sandy," she spoke up before I could answer her question. "I know you're only seeing clients part-time, but I
wish you'd listened to me and taken a longer leave."

"What for," I snapped, wishing she'd stop offering me
her advice as if I were one of her college students. "So I
can lay around the house all day and feel sorry for myself?
I hate being home." My voice quivered and I reached up to
brush away the tear sliding down my cheek. "Everything
reminds me of Frank—everywhere I turn, he's there.
Sometimes I still see him standing next to me, in his faded
Rolling Stones T-shirt, doing one of his silly Mick Jagger
impressions."

Sonia reached across the table to squeeze my hand.
"Have you thought about selling the house, moving into a
condo?"

"I suppose I should," I whispered, closing my eyes. I
pictured the day we'd first moved into our house. Frank
scooped me up in his strong, hairy arms and carried me
through the front door, as if we were newlyweds. The wait-
ress appeared setting our steaming plates of food on the
table, which forced me back to the present. I breathed in
the aroma of spicy red peppers and chicken curry.

"Aren't you going to eat?" Sonia urged as she eagerly
began to fill up every inch of her plate.

"I'm not very hungry," I admitted, reaching for the
mixed vegetables.

Sonia gave me a harsh stare, her dark, brown eyes narrowing. "Sandy, you have to eat more than that. You
already look as if you've lost weight."

"All right." I sighed, serving myself some of the chicken curry. I knew better than to argue with Professor Gonzales. I took several small bites feigning satisfaction while Sonia continued to pack it in as if she hadn't eaten in days.

After a few more mouthfuls, she paused. "Glenn says hello. He's worried about you too."

"How is he?" I asked, remembering how happy I'd felt when Sonia and Glenn had finally tied the knot. Only now, all I felt was bitterness, jealousy because I was left completely alone.

"Oh, he's fine—going crazy as usual with his students. But he absolutely loves teaching at San Martin High. Says he wouldn't teach anywhere else."

"That's good," I nodded, suddenly wishing I were Sonia.

"Maya says hello. She called last week." Her voice faltering, Sonia hesitated, then continued. "She was very sad for Tyrone and his family—Mr. Cameron had a sudden heart attack and died."

I felt the walls start to close in on me. I could hear the buildings outside begin to crumble and the sounds of the angry ocean waiting to consume me. I abruptly stood up. "I have to go," I whispered. Then I turned and rushed out the door leaving Sonia behind with a look of stark pity on her face.

∾ ∾ ∾

I was greeted by silence as I unlocked the door and went inside the small adobe house Frank and I had shared for almost a decade. The second I took my coat off and set my briefcase on the floor, my gaze fell on Frank's faded blue armchair in the corner of the living room. I imagined his long legs stretched out on the ottoman while he watched the evening news. It was his favorite spot in the house, especially when the Lakers were playing. One time I mentioned that his old armchair had started to look a little ratty and maybe it was time to get a new one. He simply retorted. "Bite your tongue, Dr. Martínez! This is my Mamba chair!"

My eyes welled with tears as I made my way into the bedroom to change. I was reaching into the closet for a warm, long-sleeved blouse, when I spotted Frank's favorite blue *guayabera* shirt he bought the summer we vacationed in Cuernavaca. I pictured him patting his lumpy stomach each time he consumed a plate of enchiladas, saying, "See, I'm a *panzón* like Diego Rivera!" Throughout our marriage, Frank had acquired a list of his favorite words in Spanish. He had even become an expert in satirical translations like *"Colitas arriba,"* for "Bottoms up." That was one of my absolute favorites and it never failed to make everyone laugh, only now I'd never hear him make that silly toast again.

As I changed into the purple Laker pajamas Frank gave to me on my last birthday, the phone began to ring. I slumped down on the edge of the bed and reluctantly picked up the receiver. It was my mother calling from Delano.

"Hija, you haven't called—I've been worried about you."

"I'm fine—just busy," I lied, wondering if that's how I would've been as a parent, always worried about my children.

"Sandra, I wish you'd waited a bit longer before going back to work."

I fought the impulse to hang up. It never failed. My mother was always trying to fix everyone's life except her own. "How's Dad?" I asked, hoping to distract her.

"*Está muy contento.* He received his five-year pin *anoche.*"

"That's good." I replied, thinking back to the struggle it had taken to convince Dad to attend A.A. meetings. It wasn't until Mom began going to Al-Anon meetings for the family member's of alcoholics on her own that he finally agreed to get help. He'd been going to A.A. for years now and had even made some friends there.

"When are you coming to visit?"

"I'm not sure," I answered, flooded by memories of the first time Frank had gone with me to visit my parents in Delano. He surprised me when he began quoting one historical fact after another about César Chávez and the UFW. For a *gringo* from a wealthy Southern California family, Frank was well-informed and open-minded about the farmworker struggle.

"*Hija,*" my mother's voice interjected, "you're going to be all right—it takes time to heal." Pausing for a second, her voice grew hoarse. "There isn't a day that goes by that I don't think of Andrés."

Mom rarely talked about my younger brother Andy's tragic death. Whenever Dad and I mentioned Andy, she quickly found an excuse to leave the room, but Frank's sudden death was making us relive it all.

"I have to go," I blurted out, hanging up the phone before she had time to react. I took a long deep breath, collapsing onto the bed as I buried my face in Frank's pillow. I cried softly for Frank and for all our unfulfilled dreams, the trip to Greece that we often talked about, the children we would never have. He made me smile every time he talked about wanting a daughter who looked like me: brown eyes and caramel skin, not pale like him, but I'd failed him miserably. After two miscarriages we'd talked about adopting, but became busy, Frank with his tax business and me with my private practice. Now it was too damn late. Frank was gone. All I had left were guilt and regrets. Maybe Sonia was right. Maybe I *should* sell the house and get rid of all these damn memories.

FIVE
Dr. Martínez

That night, I cried myself to sleep, but by eight o'clock the next morning I was back in my office staring at the files on my desk. As I took a sip of my coffee, I thought about the mornings when Frank would surprise me with a cup of espresso in bed before he left for work. I warned Frank to watch out because he was spoiling me rotten, but he always fired back with, "That's what your hunk of burning love is supposed to do!"

My eyes blurred with tears as I gazed at Frank's handsome face in the photo on my desk, his sea-blue eyes and golden curly hair. We'd taken that picture on our first trip to San Francisco to celebrate our third anniversary. Frank had asked another tourist to take our picture while we posed in front of the huge Christmas tree in Union Square. That entire weekend, Frank went wild snapping one picture after another as we rode the trolley cars and walked around Fisherman's Wharf.

I felt the twinges of familiar guilt penetrating my body. Why hadn't Frank confided in me, talked to me about his depression? I was his wife, his best friend. For the longest time, he'd been aloof, distant, looking for any excuse to get away by himself. He spent more time at his office and he often didn't get home until after dark. My first thoughts were that he was seeing someone else or that perhaps he was in some financial mess with his business. If only I'd known that he was severely depressed. If only he'd reached out to me. I was the trained psychologist who was supposed to help others.

The police had called that morning to say that one of the motel maids had found Frank dead in his hotel room. I went into complete shock when they went on to explain that it was from a drug overdose. I kept repeating to myself that this couldn't possibly be true, that it was all a terrible mistake. Frank had left the night before to meet with a client in Santa Barbara. I tried talking him into letting me go along, that it could serve as a second honeymoon. But Frank had refused in a dry, humorless voice, repeating that it was only an overnight trip. He made it seem like I had no choice but to let him go, as if time alone was exactly what he needed.

I blotted my eyes. If only I'd insisted on going with him on that trip, then maybe he'd still be alive. All the signs were there. Why had I ignored them? Could it be that Frank's mother had been right? I still hear her accusations ringing in my head that day on the telephone, "Tell me, Sandra. How is it you didn't suspect anything? Were you so damn preoccupied with your practice that you ignored my son's feelings?" I had tried to defend myself, telling her she was wrong, that if anyone had adored Frank, it was me. She refused to listen and hung up on me. We didn't speak again until the day of the funeral where she managed to restrain her anger in front of my parents. It wasn't until they were lowering his casket into the ground and we both began to sob fiercely that I understood why she had lashed out at me. She loved Frank as much as I did and we'd never see him again. I went home right after the funeral, refusing to attend the customary reception with family and friends. That night, I took several sedatives the doctor had given me, but I knew nothing would ever stop the bleeding in my heart. Nor was I willing to join Frank, not yet.

Leaning back in my chair, I closed my eyes for a few seconds. Why couldn't I stop blaming myself for Frank's death? All these years of telling my clients that guilt was poisonous and now I was doing just that. As I placed my hand on my gold wedding band and caressed it, the light on my phone started to blink. It was the receptionist.

"Dr. Martínez," Katie exclaimed, "there's a young man here to see you. He said he doesn't have an appointment, but he wants to know if you can talk, even if it's if only for five minutes."

"His name?"

"Tyrone, that's all he said."

I glanced at my calendar. My next appointment wasn't scheduled to arrive for another half hour. "Give me a minute, then send him in."

"Will do," Katie replied.

Breathing in slowly, I turned to gaze out the window. It was a clear November day and there was a solitary bird perched on the Azalea tree in the small backyard. I imagined myself at its side, desolate and alone. Would I ever be able recover the confidence and strength that I'd once felt with Frank at my side?

There were several light taps on the door and I turned around to find Tyrone Cameron peering at me through the cracked door. My eyebrows shot up in surprise as he stepped inside my office.

"Hi, Ms. Martínez." He smiled as I went over to his side and we embraced.

It had been years since I'd last seen Tyrone. He was several inches taller with striking features that reminded me of a young Denzel Washington.

"Thanks for seeing me."

"You're very welcome," I said, doing my best to act light and carefree. "Have a seat. It's been a long time."

He grinned, taking the empty chair across from my desk. "I'm a big-time college guy now."

"So I heard. And how is Maya?"

"Good, real good, actually. She hasn't traded me in yet for one of those Ivy league types at Stanford."

There was a momentary pause as his smile faded. "Maya told me about Frank—I'm sorry."

I inhaled slowly. "I'm sorry about your father, too," I gently offered.

"Yeah, it was a heart attack." Then he suddenly leaned forward, raising his voice to say, "But as soon as I graduate, I'll get Momma that house Dad always talked about buying for her."

"I'm sure you will," I agreed, as my mind flashed back to the last time I saw Mr. and Mrs. Cameron at Roosevelt for Senior Award Night. I would never forget the look of pride on their faces when Tyrone had gone on stage to accept his award.

"And this summer I'm getting an internship at a local agency. I'm determined to become the best counselor ever so I can help others just like you and Mr. G."

"That's amazing," I nodded, wondering if I could ever inspire anyone again. It was all I could do now to force myself out of bed each morning, pretend that everything was fine.

"But the reason I'm here, Ms. Martínez," Tyrone said, interrupting my thoughts, "is because Maya said I should come talk to you. It's about my sister Zakiya."

"Zakiya," I whispered softly, thinking back to that day in their apartment when I had asked Zakiya about the origin of her name, telling her it was uniquely beautiful. A huge smile had spread across Zakiya's face as she proudly explained that it was a Swahili word that means intelligent.

"Zakiya's been real depressed. Won't talk to anyone and she's fighting with Momma all the time. So I was wondering if maybe you could help her like you did that time for me."

I felt Tyrone's eyes burn into me and for an instant, I imagined myself telling him to get out of my office, to find help somewhere else. Couldn't he see that I wasn't the same Dr. Martínez who had once helped him and his friends?

Feeling an uneasiness filter through my body, I said, "I'm not sure if I can now—I'm only working half days."

Tyrone wasn't about to give up, his voice pleading with me. "Please think about it, Ms. Martínez. I know it's a hard time for you now, but if anyone can help Zakiya, it's you. We're still living in the same apartment—maybe you could come by one afternoon."

Staring into his huge dark eyes, I wondered how I could possibly make him understand that I didn't know if I had enough strength to save anybody except myself. Before I could formulate another excuse, Tyrone was on his feet.

"I have a class next hour, so I have to go, but please, Ms. Martínez, think about it. I know you can help Zee like you once helped me."

As the door closed behind him, I was plagued with more doubts and fears. How could I console another human being when I was struggling to cope with Frank's sudden death? Picking up our photograph, I stared into Frank's eyes, shaking my head. No, Tyrone shouldn't have come to see me. I was the last person in the world who could help Zakiya.

SIX
Zakiya

It's my first week back at school and nothing seems the same as before. The faces I once recognized seem distorted. I make small talk on the school bus with everyone, but when I get to my classes, I'm unable to concentrate on what the teachers are saying. Performing Arts, which was once my favorite class, seems like a total waste. My hand used to be the first one to go up when Mrs. Jessup asked for a volunteer for one of her new dance steps, but now my body feels heavy like a tree trunk. Dalana is the first one to notice the change in me.

"No hand in the air? That's not the Zakiya I know." The look on her face matches the playful tone of her voice.

"*You're* the teacher's pet. Not me," I reply in a dry sarcastic tone, hoping she'll get off my back.

Dalana's eyes burn into me. "Suit yourself, Sis."

After that, she doesn't speak to me again, but I couldn't care less. When third period ends, I go straight to the library instead of having lunch. I find an empty table way in the back where I pretend to work on an essay for World Lit. The truth is I don't want to be around anyone, not even Peyton. All I want is to be left alone, to avoid more fake words of sympathy from students and teachers who act as if they really care.

I'm headed for my locker when I come face to face with Peyton in the hallway. I'm forced to pause in my steps. "Hey, where were you?" she asks, shifting her backpack to her other shoulder. "I waited for you so we could have lunch?"

"Had to go to the library," I explain, stepping around her and continuing down the hallway, but Peyton turns around and follows me to my locker.

As I reach inside for my Spanish book, she says, "There's a volleyball meeting today—you're coming, right?"

I shrug my shoulders as she leans in closer, her eyes locked in on me. "Coach was asking for you."

"So?" I tell her, slamming my locker door shut and fleeing toward the hallway.

Trailing after me like a sheep dog, she asks, "Why can't you make it to the meeting?"

"It's Momma, she needs my help today," I reluctantly answer, realizing that I've always disliked people who lie and here I am doing just that.

"Suit yourself," Peyton retorts as I quicken my step, leaving her behind.

The second I walk into Spanish class, Carlos is at my side. In that sweet romantic voice of his, he says, "*Señorita*, glad you're back—we all missed you."

I stare at his handsome face, the words stuck in my throat. Just then, Mr. Villamil orders everyone to take their seats and open their books to Chapter Five. Carlos hurries back to his seat. I can feel his eyes on me as Mr. Villamil reviews the commands in Spanish, but I refuse to glance his way. When Mr. Villamil has everyone pair up to work on the commands, I turn my back to Carlos and move toward Mike Johnson, whose Spanish is not only worse than mine, but his underarms stink.

As soon as the fifth period bell rings, I grab my books and hurry toward the door. Out of the corner of my eye, I catch a glimpse of Carlos. There's a sad expression on his face that lets me know I've hurt his feelings. For a second, I feel guilty, but I erase the thought from my mind. It's not like he's my boyfriend anyway. Avoiding my locker, I head in the opposite direction of the main quad away from the ugly yellow school buses that are already lined and waiting. The sound of honking cars and noisy students doesn't distract me as I hurry across campus through the back parking lot. When I come to the stoplight at the corner, I cross the street into the wealthy neighborhoods near the school. I continue walking until Roosevelt High is completely out of sight. After about five minutes, I come to the small shopping mall where Discount Foods is located.

I gaze at the familiar grocery store front. The huge red sign above the automatic door opens and closes while customers go in and out with their grocery carts. I picture the first time Dad took me with him to pick up his paycheck. His eyes glittered with excitement as he bragged to his co-workers, "This here's my baby girl." Dad was always cheerful and talkative, got along with everyone. He never complained about anything, not even when he had to work on Saturdays. I always wondered how he and Momma could be so different.

Blinking back the tears, I whisper to myself, "Why'd you have to go and die on me?" I turn around and walk away from the shopping mall until it's completely out of sight. Pausing to glance at my cell phone, I suddenly realize I need to get home before Momma gets suspicious. I spot a bus stop at the next corner, so I quicken my pace and make it there just as the city bus pulls up. I pick an empty seat next to the window. When my phone beeps, I pull it out of my pocket. It's another text from Peyton. Ignoring it, I gaze through the window at the busy traffic, the familiar office buildings and mobile parks. When the city bus pulls over at the bus stop in front of the cemetery, I feel a wrenching in my heart. Leaning my head against the window, I'm tempted to race to Dad's side so I can talk with him, be with him again. Only the bus door quickly opens and closes behind a little old lady carrying a heavy bag. My voice heavy with grief, I whisper, "Daddy, I'm sorry."

The minute I walk through the front door, Momma hollers at me from the couch. "Girl, where have you been?"

"Volleyball meeting," I lie, for the second time today.

"We're having leftovers tonight. Tyrone won't be home until late."

"I'm not hungry," I answer. Just as I am about to head for the stairs, I notice the pile of Dad's shirts and pants on the couch next to Momma. She appears to be sorting through them before she places them in the cardboard box on the floor. I feel like my mind is swept away by explosive anger. "Momma, what do you think you're doing?"

Her shoulders stiffening, Momma reaches for Dad's favorite blue and grey Dodgers jersey. "I'm giving them to the Goodwill."

The next thing I know, I'm jerking Dad's jersey out of her clumsy hands. Then I rush upstairs to my bedroom, closing the door behind me. I let my backpack slide to the floor and fling myself on the bed, holding Dad's jersey tightly against my chest. It still smells like him. Closing my eyes, I imagine him sitting in his favorite chair downstairs while he watched the Dodgers' game, repeating the same words to me, "Zee baby, you better believe we're gonna win." Then he would raise his cup of coffee high in the air and we would both cheer, "Go Dodgers!"

How could Momma even think of getting rid of Dad's things? I angrily think to myself, rubbing Dad's Dodgers jersey against my face. My mind flashes back to the cemetery and suddenly I'm drowning. My phone beeps just then as Peyton texts, *I need to talk to you.* I turn my phone off, wondering why she keeps nagging me. Why can't everyone just leave me alone?

Later that evening, I hear a light tap on my door. "Zee, are you still up?"

It's Tyrone. I can hear Jerome's music blasting from across the hallway as he cracks the door open and repeats his question. Pretending I'm asleep, I don't answer him, so Tyrone closes the door softly and leaves. I'm glad he left. I don't have anything to say to him. How can he possibly understand how empty and alone I feel inside? He's got his college dreams, his college friends, but me, I don't have anyone or anything anymore.

I reach for Dad's jersey and squeeze it tightly against my chest. If only I could have one more day with him, feel his arms around me while he tells me how beautiful I am, that I can make all my dreams come true, be a dancer, be anything I want. If only I could wake up in the morning and everything would be the same as before.

SEVEN
Zakiya

The next morning, I wait until I'm sure Jerome has left before getting dressed. I quietly go into the kitchen, relieved Momma's already left for the hospital. The last thing I want is for her to bug me about skipping breakfast. I reach in the cupboard for a granola bar to eat on the bus just as Tyrone appears behind me.

"Hey, Zee, I knocked on your door last night, but I guess you were asleep."

There are dark circles under his eyes as if he hasn't slept in days. His backpack seems to hang from his slumped shoulders. "Yeah, I was," I mumble, turning to leave, but he's quick to follow me.

"Wait up. I'll give you a ride—my class was cancelled."

With his gaze on me, I try to steady my voice, explaining that I promised a friend on the bus that I'd help her with some homework, but Tyrone doesn't fall for it. "Come on, Zee. Isn't my car better than the bus?"

"All right," I reluctantly agree, following him out the front door. It's a hazy morning and the smell of Mrs. Pantoja's homemade *tortillas* floats in the air as we make our way downstairs. While we cross the street to where

Tyrone's green Honda is parked, I'm instantly struck with sadness. I imagine Dad's face the day he surprised Tyrone with it, handing him the car keys. "Son, you need your own car now that you're going to the university." Tyrone was speechless. It had taken him years to forgive Dad for leaving Momma that time, but that day every inch of his face shone with pride and respect.

Wiping away a single tear, I climb into the front seat and Tyrone pulls away from the curb before the school bus can beat him. After a very long minute, he finally glances over at me. "I saw Ms. Martínez the other day. She might come by sometime."

My lips are quivering as I raise my voice to say, "I don't need a shrink if that's what you're thinking. Besides, didn't her husband just kill himself? Maybe she's the one who needs help."

Tyrone's voice is low and sad, "He did."

"Jeez, okay, we won't talk about that."

There is a long moment of silence, then Tyrone asks, "How's Peyton?"

"She's fine," I answer, feeling more relaxed now that he's decided not to bring up Ms. Martínez again.

When Tyrone finally pulls into the parking lot to drop me off, there is a warm, caring look in his eyes. "You wanna hang out this weekend. Maybe go see a movie?"

Our eyes meet and for a second, I feel as if I'm staring at Dad. I feel a sudden impulse to move closer, to lay my head on his shoulder like I used to do with Dad anytime I was feeling awful. Reaching for the door handle, I whisper, "I can't." Then I hurry out of the car, but not before I notice the shadow spreading across his face.

Just as I approach the main quad, I catch a glimpse of Peyton standing with a group of girls. I quicken my pace, hoping she won't notice me, but no such luck. She hurries to catch up with me. "Wait, Zakiya. Why haven't you answered my texts?"

Avoiding her, I refuse to slow down, but Peyton is persistent. She tugs at my backpack, forcing me to stop. "I was busy."

"Oh, yeah, doing what?"

I glare at her pale and hollow cheeks. "None of your business."

"Whatever," she hisses at me, as I continue through the busy hallway toward my locker.

During English, when Mrs. Harrison asks me to explain the use of metaphor in the Blake poem we're reading, I jerk my head up, unable to provide her with an answer. Mrs. Harrison narrows her eyes in disbelief since I'm always the first one to raise my hand when we're analyzing poetry. When I continue to remain mute, she turns to another student while I make a futile attempt to listen to the classroom discussion.

When it's time for Performing Arts, I don't bother to change into my yoga pants. Faking several coughs, I explain to Mrs. Jessup that I don't feel well, so she instructs me to sit and take notes while she reviews the Pas-de-bourrée with the class. I'm sitting in the back, pretending to write in my dance notebook when Dalana inches over to my side. "Liar," she whispers, as Mrs. Jessup orders everyone on their feet to try the new three step movement she's just demonstrated.

"Shut your face!" I warn Dalana as she turns to join the class. Like a stick of dynamite ready to explode, I grab my backpack and flee from the gym before Mrs. Harrison has time to notice. I hurry out of the gym, tears running down my cheeks, and into the liberal arts building where I find the nearest bathroom. I'll hide there until the lunch bell rings, the last thing I want is for anyone to see me crying. I slam my palm against a stall door and it swings open. I'm shocked to see that a chunky, white girl is in there, she's not sitting down, she's standing, her head is bent down and her right sleeve is rolled up. She's holding a pair of manicure scissors and blood is trickling from a cut on her forearm. It's then that I notice that she has many small scars below her elbow.

"Get out!" she yells, raising her face to me, eyes flashing with rage. It's Becky, I recognize her, she was a year ahead of me in middle school. Now she hangs out with a group of other white girls that are always in detention.

∾ ∾ ∾

"I didn't know," I stammer, backing out of the stall.

It looks like she might use the scissors on me, but then her gaze softens. She puts her scissors back in her leather manicure kit which sits open on the toilet paper dispenser and unspools some T.P. and hands it to me. "Looks like you need this as bad as I do."

"Thanks," I say. Wiping the tears from my face as she wipes the blood from her arm with some toilet paper and gets a bandage she's stashed in her manicure kit. "You okay?" I ask. My voice hushed with pity.

"You and your pity can go to hell," she says with a cruel chuckle.

"Oh, I'm already there," I say. I hear myself laughing. It's the first time I've laughed since Dad died. "I'm getting outta here. This place makes me sick. You wanna come?" she asks, drying her hands.

I hesitate for a moment, thinking back to all the warnings I've heard about her and her friends who wear heavy black eye make-up, that they're severely depressed and will drag you down with them. But then again, why the hell should I care about what other people say. "I've never skipped before," I finally admit.

A confident smile spreads across Becky's round face. "There's always a first time. Come on, let's go," she says, as I follow her out of the bathroom. We carefully sneak out of the building and around the gym, past the empty football field toward the south side of campus. I can feel the fear mounting inside as I imagine a police officer chasing after me. If there's anything Momma and Dad taught us since we were little, it was to never run from the cops.

My fears begin to subside once we're far enough away from the school buildings. Taking a deep breath, I pause at Becky's side, asking, "Where exactly are we going?"

"There's this park where I hang out over by the train station," she answers. "It's pretty empty, some homeless people there, but they don't bother you."

After ten more minutes of walking, we come to a small park several blocks away from the train station. I can hear the sound of train whistles going by as we cross the street into the park. "Let's sit over here," Becky says, pointing to a spot behind the bathrooms. Once we're sitting on the cool grass, Becky says, "This is way better than the girls bathroom, right?"

"Lots better," I say. We talk about Roosevelt. How fake everyone acts. We talk about hip-hop too, she likes Anville, like me, but she also listens to emo rappers like Lil Peep. Finally, I work up the courage to ask her if it hurts when she cuts herself.

Shaking her head, Becky confesses, "It feels good."

"Can't you try something else, like getting drunk?"

"It's not the same," Becky explains. Then she takes out a sandwich from her backpack and begins to eat. I'm left speechless, wondering how in the world she can eat so casually after what I just saw her do an hour ago.

We hang out at the park listening to music and talking about lame teachers until we realize it's almost three o'clock. On her feet, Becky says, "I gotta go. My stepmom will be so pissed if I'm not home by three-thirty. Let me know when you wanna hang out."

"Yeah, thanks," I answer, sensing I need to get my own butt home before Momma freaks out.

I catch the city bus on the other side of the park and fifteen minutes later, it drops me off on the corner near our apartment building. My stomach is all tangled up inside. As soon as I open the front door, Momma rushes up to me, slapping me hard on the face.

"Where the hell have you been, Zakiya? Now don't lie to me and tell me you were at school 'cause I know you ditched your classes.

"Get away from me!" I holler back at her, turning toward the stairway, only Momma is right behind me.

"The school called, said you weren't in your classes, so no more lies!"

Taking two steps at a time, I race upstairs to my room, locking the door behind me. I can still hear Momma's screams in the hallway, so I turn up the music on my phone, drowning out her hysterical voice.

Several hours later, I hear a light knocking on my door. It's Tyrone pleading with me to let him come inside. "Zee, we need to talk. Momma told me what happened."

If anyone really cares about me, it's Tyrone. I get up from the bed and unlock the door.

"Thanks, Zee," he says, relief in his voice as he sits on the edge of my bed.

"Why can't Momma ever keep her big mouth shut?"

"She's just trying to help," he gently explains. "Have you even thought about the consequences of your actions? You could get suspended."

I let out a bitter laugh. "What do I care?"

Tyrone leans forward, placing his hand over mine. "You don't mean that, do you? Don't you remember how much Dad wanted us both to get a college degree?"

I yank my hand away from him, shouting, "Get out, Tyrone—you don't know anything. Get out now!"

"Suit yourself," he says, his words heavy with grief.

As soon as I lock the door behind him, I bury my face in my pillow, tears streaming down my face. Why did I have to yell at Tyrone that way? He was only trying to help. If only I could talk to Dad, if only he were here to hold me and tell me everything's gonna be alright.

EIGHT
Zakiya

The next day is like a nightmare. Momma insists on taking the morning off from work so we can meet with my counselor, and if that isn't bad enough, she dresses in the frumpy green suit she wears to church on Sundays. When we arrive at the counselling office, Mr. Mellon's door is wide open. The moment he sees us, he comes over to shake Momma's hand and tells us to take a seat in his office. He explains that since this is my first time ditching, I'll only receive lunch suspension. "Zakiya's always been a great student," he reassures Momma, who breathes a sigh of relief. Then he goes over my missed assignments. When Mr. Mellon looks into my eyes, asking if there's anything I want to talk about, I feel my neck muscles stiffen. Before I can respond, Momma confesses in a thick, uneven voice, "It's been very difficult having to adjust to a new life without Zakiya's dad."

Feeling waves of anger inside of me, I want to reach out and cover her mouth with my hand. A new life. Momma's crazy. I don't want a new life. I want my old one back. With Dad! How can she even say that?

With eyes full of sympathy, Mr. Mellon nods. "Yes, I understand—I'm very sorry for your loss." Focusing his gaze on me again, he says, "Zakiya, please remember, if at any time you need to talk, that's what I'm here for." Then he turns to Momma and tells her that he will look out for me. In that exact moment, I want to shout at them to leave me alone, to mind their own business, but I know I can't. Instead, I mumble a fake thank you as Mr. Mellon gives me the classroom number for lunch detention. By now, Momma is on her feet, thanking him again and again.

Once we're alone in the main quad and I'm about to escape from Momma, she clutches my arm firmly. "Now listen here, you make sure you come home on the bus right after school." Glaring back at her, I jerk my arm free from her grasp and hurry to change into my yoga pants for Performing Arts.

The moment I step onto the gym floor, Dalana walks up to me, an ugly scowl on her face. Her lips parting, she says, "Heard you ditched yesterday? Did you get caught?"

"None of your business," I reply, stepping around her so that I can hand Mrs. Jessup my pass.

"Glad you're back," she smiles as I quickly move to the other side of the gym to do my warm-up. I have to stay as far away as possible from Dalana and her big mouth. She really knows how to piss me off. I never ask her any questions about her Prison Dad so why the hell is she being so damn nosey with me?

After about ten minutes, Mrs. Jessup instructs us to sit down and take notes in our notebooks while we watch a video on the history of Jazz. I can feel Dalana eyeing me as I pick a spot on the bleachers behind all the other students.

Once the video begins, I forget all about Dalana. The video is so cool. It's about some of the greatest Jazz musicians and singers like Miles Davis and Billie Holiday. But when Louis Armstrong comes on, thoughts of Dad begin to swirl in my head. I must've been around four or five years old when Momma got real sick with the flu so Dad had to give me my bath. He brought his small radio into the bathroom and gave me a bath to the sounds of Louis Armstrong. I never gave it much thought before, but maybe that's why I love music and dance so much. The dark hole in my heart begins to widen when the bell rings and Mrs. Jessup is forced to stop the video. I breathe a sigh of relief for the last thing I want to do is let anyone see me cry.

At noon, I'm on my way to detention but Peyton stops me in the hallway. "Heard about your detention."

"Yeah, so what?"

Rolling her eyes, Peyton asks, "Can I meet you by your locker after school for volleyball? It's about next season."

"No, I'm done with that."

Peyton's eyes bust out of their sockets. "What? Why?"

"Volleyball sucks, that's why."

I see flames blazing in Peyton's eyes. Her words sharp as knives, she says, "Go ahead, suit yourself. I hear you're hanging out with Becky now." Then she rushes off to catch up with another one of her volleyball friends. This time I know that I've really pissed her off, but why the hell should I care what she thinks anyway?

Lunch detention isn't so messed up after all since there are only two other students besides me. I'm very surprised that Becky isn't one of them, but maybe she's been suspended. When the teacher's aide hands us our make-up work, she warns that we're not allowed to talk unless there are questions about our assignments. I only missed two classes, so I finish quickly and I spend the rest of the time munching on my granola bar until the bell rings. By the time I get to Spanish class, I'm feeling very uneasy about seeing Carlos again but he doesn't even seem to notice me. As I walk down the aisle, he turns his back to me and begins talking to the nerdy guy behind him. A few minutes later, when Mr. Villamil asks us to form groups to practice the verb *gustar*, Carlos rushes off to pair up with the pretty girl in the front row. I feel a slight twinge of jealousy, but I suppose that's what I deserve. I treated him like crap the other day.

After school, I go straight home on the school bus, but the second Momma sees me, she begins shouting orders at me as if she were an Army captain: "Zakiya, take the trash out. Zakiya, take the clothes out of the dryer and fold them. . . ." She's on me like a vulture until I insist I have lots of homework. Only then does she back off, so I escape to my bedroom. But what's even more disgusting is that when Jerome gets home, he acts pissy just like Momma. He cracks my door open until I can see his creepy egg-shaped head.

"What, no ditching today?" he asks tauntingly.

"Keep your ugly mouth shut!" I warn him, hurrying to lock my door as he disappears down the hallway.

The only one who doesn't throw anything in my face is Tyrone. When we're all seated at the dinner table that night and Momma tells him about the school visit, he turns to me, saying, "You got lucky, Zee." His voice is gentle and loving just like Dad's. But my warm feeling disappears when Momma lets out a chuckle.

"And it better stay like that or else," she says, giving me one of her sarcastic looks. Then she fixes her gaze on Tyrone. "Son, I'm gonna ask my supervisor tomorrow if I can go back to work full-time. The rent's going up soon and we're gonna need the money now that your daddy's gone."

"Does that mean I'll get a bigger allowance?" Jerome asks, jerking his head up from where he's been peering down into his lap attempting to conceal his cell phone.

Momma is quick to notice, only she doesn't holler at him like she does with me. "Son, I told you not to bring that thing to the table."

"Sorry, Momma," he mutters, putting it away in his pocket.

I want to holler at Jerome that he's a selfish little punk, but Tyrone beats me to it. "Is that all you ever think about?" he asks in a loud scolding voice. Then he turns to look at Momma, his words heavy with concern. "Momma, you don't have to do that. I can get a part-time job."

"Son," Momma says, shaking her head fiercely, "You got enough to do already with all those classes. Besides, I like my job at the hospital."

I'm instantly taken back to that day Dad told us he had gotten his promotion at Discount Foods. His face was bright with joy as he told Momma she could cut back to part-time work. Momma tried and tried to talk Dad out of it, reminding him they were saving up for a house, but Dad wouldn't hear of it.

"Please think about it, Momma," Tyrone insists, but Momma ignores him, standing up and going over to the stove to refill the gravy bowl. This whole conversation makes my stomach feel like it's tied up in knots. Back upstairs in my room that night, a thousand terrifying thoughts begin to swirl in my head. What if they won't give Momma full-time work again? What if we have to move somewhere else, to another city? What if I have to leave Roosevelt? We can't possibly leave Dad here with no one to visit him. Trying to calm myself, I reach inside the drawer of my nightstand for the picture of me and Dad. It was taken on my 7th birthday at Tomol Beach. Dad was wearing his silly straw hat and he had his arm around me as we posed in front of the sandcastle we'd just built. My body trembling, I shove the photograph back in the drawer. Then I begin to pace in circles around the room, only nothing seems to help as the pounding in my head continues to grow louder and louder. Sinking onto the carpet, I cover my face with my hands and I begin to cry fiercely, my body shaking with fear. The pounding in my head keeps getting louder and louder as I whisper, "Why'd you have to go and die on me, Dad? What about all the promises you made to us?" It is then that I think of Becky, the tiny scars on her arms, the relief on her face. I pull my body off the floor and I reach for my backpack on the bed. My hand trembling, I take out a paper clip and unbend it, gently pricking at my left arm until trickles of blood begin to appear. I continue to pierce my skin until my anxiety slowly begins to diminish. Closing my eyes, I release several deep breaths, aware that I'm feeling calm, that the pounding in my head is gone.

Becky was right—it does feel good.

NINE
Dr. Martínez

As I turned into Tyrone's apartment building, I wondered why I let Sonia know about Tyrone's unexpected visit to my office. She went on and on about how each time Maya called from Stanford, all she would talk about was how worried Tyrone was about Zakiya. I'd tried changing the conversation with Sonia, but that had only made things worse. She had reminded me of why I had gone into counselling in the first place and how we both were committed to helping communities of color. I didn't want to admit it, but I knew she was right.

Casting a quick glance at the newly painted low-income housing units, I descended from the car and headed toward the familiar apartment. It took several minutes before the door was opened and I found myself face-to-face with Mrs. Cameron. Her lips parted in a smile that spread across her face. She looked the same as when I'd last seen her, except for a few streaks of grey that filtered through her thick hair.

"Dr. Martínez," she gasped, "what a surprise—please come in."

As I stepped inside the small living room, I couldn't help but notice the tall, stoic Black man who rose from the couch and moved to our side.

"Dr. Martínez," Mrs. Cameron began, "This is Father Brown, from our parish."

"I'm very pleased to meet you," he said, towering above me. When he reached out with his long slender fingers to shake my hand, I noticed the white clerical collar barely visible underneath his blue cotton shirt. I tried to hide my surprise as we shook hands for it was the first time I'd met an African American Catholic priest in this area.

Turning back to Mrs. Cameron, Father Brown said, "Martha, I need to get going now, I'll come by another day. But remember what we talked about—you must have faith." Then he patted her on the hand, before shaking my hand once more before he left.

As soon as we were both seated on the couch, I promptly spoke up. "I'm sorry for interrupting your visit with Father Brown."

Her words heavy with sadness, she nodded. "Father Brown's been by every week. You see, Jerry and I never missed Sunday Mass." Her voice faltered for a second. "I'm sure you heard about my Jerry."

"Yes, I'm sorry," I whispered, as she reached up to wipe a tear from the corner of her eye.

I could feel a sudden tightening in my throat. "I recently lost my own husband," I admitted in an uneven voice.

"Yes, Tyrone told me—I'm sorry," she nodded, her voice growing dim. "I'm sure you must know what I've been going through." Pausing for a moment, she swallowed hard. "You see, Jerry and I met when I was only sixteen and he never let me go after that. That man followed me every-where. Back then, it wasn't like now. If you was a girl you couldn't go out at all. I know because my daddy wouldn't let my sister and I go out alone. But that Jerry was some-thing. He never gave up, found the most creative ways to see me. One time he came straight up to the door to see if he could get permission to take me out. Lucky for him, Momma answered or my daddy would've given him a good whippin'."

Mrs. Cameron chuckled, reaching for a handkerchief from her pocket to dab at her eyes. I reached out to pat her on the hand, knowing exactly how lonely she must be feel-ing, but at least she had his children. My miscarriages came rushing into my thoughts. I looked away for a second at the framed Virgin Mary on the wall wondering if she would be able to help us both.

"I thought we'd see our grandchildren grown," she snif-fled. "But I guess the good Lord had to take him."

Her next question took me by complete surprise. Rais-ing her head slightly, she asked, "Was your husband sick too?"

I swallowed hard, wondering if Mrs. Cameron was right. Maybe it had been a sickness of the heart that had taken Frank's life just like with Mr. Cameron. "Yes, I guess you could say Frank was sick too," I softly replied, trying to push away the confusing thoughts in my head. "But if you don't mind, I'd like to talk about the reason for my visit. Tyrone came to see me last week and he told me how worried he is about Zakiya."

Her thick eyebrows shot up. "He did? That doesn't sur-prise me. Tyrone and Zakiya have always been close, she won't talk to nobody except him. But, lately, she's been misbehavin'—she even took off from school the other day. I had to go see the school counselor with her. She almost got herself kicked out."

Mrs. Cameron crossed and uncrossed her legs.

"That's why I'm here," I offered reassuringly. "I was wondering if perhaps Zakiya would agree to talk with me." Mrs. Cameron's eyes glistened with hope. "Lord Jesus, that would certainly help. She used to be such a sweet child. I've about had it with all her back talking, but I'm very worried about her."

Just then, the front door opened and Zakiya walked into the living room. She froze in her steps when she saw me on the couch.

"Now don't just stand there," Mrs. Cameron said, motioning for her to come closer. "Dr. Martínez came by to visit. Girl, I'm talking to you. I know you remember her."

Zakiya took one step closer, mumbling a feeble hello. I could tell by her body language and the strained look on her face that she was not at all pleased by my unexpected visit. She mumbled her words as if she could hardly be bothered to say them. "Sorry, I have tons of homework."

Clutching her backpack tightly against her, she was about to head for the stairway when Mrs. Cameron raised her voice. "Girl, you ain't going nowhere," she demanded. "Dr. Martínez wants to ask you a question."

There were dark streaks of anger in Zakiya's eyes as she gazed at me. "Yeah, like what?"

"I was wondering if you would be willing to come by my office so we could talk."

"There's nothing to talk about," she fired back.

Mrs. Cameron was on her feet now, pointing her index finger at Zakiya. "Shh—no need to act so high and mighty. If Dr. Martínez was nice enough to come all the way over here to see you, you're gonna be respectful."

Her eyes flinching, Zakiya was defiant. "I don't need to talk to anybody."

I could feel the heat rising in the room. "How about just one visit?" I carefully intervened. "You can ask Tyrone— I'm not so bad to be around."

Aware of her mother's menacing stare, Zakiya rolled her eyes. "Fine." Turning to glare at her mother, she hollered, "There, are you satisfied now?" Then she hurried upstairs while Mrs. Cameron shook her head in disgust.

Sitting back down on the couch, she continued to shake her head, but gently. "I'm so sorry, Dr. Martínez."

"No need to apologize," I reassured her. "The important thing is that Zakiya agreed to see me. I'll go ahead and set up an appointment for this week after school. Reaching for my briefcase, I handed her my card. "Here are both my numbers in case you need to contact me."

"That's real good of you," Mrs. Cameron agreed as I stood up to leave. "And I'll make sure she's there."

Walking back to my car, I thought about Zakiya and also about the words of Father Brown. The exact same words my mother had repeated to me the day of Frank's funeral. "You must have faith. You must have faith." If only it were that easy.

TEN
Dr. Martínez

Mornings were still the worst even though I was back in my office meeting with clients. I'd wake up between four and five a.m. and my mind would fill with regrets. Regrets about Frank, about what I hadn't done right, about what I could've done better. It wasn't until I'd finally drag myself out of bed to listen to NPR that I realized my life wasn't so bad. Babies being torn from their immigrant parents' arms and placed in tent cities or modern-day concentration camps. Then another Trayvon Martin, another Black man shot in the back. *How dare I feel sorry for myself?* If Frank were still alive, he would agree with me, he'd be right there standing with all the protestors. Lately, I'd even found myself talking to Frank out loud. As I opened my closet door, I'd ask him what I should wear today. When I opened the refrigerator door, I'd ask him whether I should make a sandwich or spaghetti for dinner. When I reached for the letters inside the mailbox, I'd say, "Well, Frank, is it our lucky day?" I often wondered if people heard me and thought I was losing it, but I really didn't care. Talking to Frank made me feel better.

By Thursday, I was feeling slightly more hopeful because later I'd have my first appointment with Zakiya. The morning went by quickly as I met with my first two clients. Christina was the mother of a gay teenager and she was finding it difficult to accept her son's sexuality given her devout Christian values. I couldn't help but think of Mrs. Montoya, Tommy's mother, and how she had struggled with her own Catholic beliefs when she had finally faced the reality of having a gay son. It had been difficult and painful for the entire family, but most all for Tommy's father. Christina was having the same issues with her husband.

My second appointment was especially draining. It was with Sherry, a fifty-year-old divorced woman who suffered from bouts of depression. Although Sherry had completed several degrees, she was afraid to change jobs and move to another city. Fear was slowly eating her insides and talking with her made me aware of my own fears. *Is that how I would end up, alone and miserable?* No, of course not— I'll never let that happen to me.

At noon, I decided to take my sandwich outside to the patio in the back of my office. I sat by the fountain and listened to the melody of the water, feeling the tension leave my body. I breathed in the sweet smell of lilacs from the small tree near the wooden fence. When a tiny hummingbird appeared, flying backward and forward from one branch to the next, I remembered the trip Frank and I took to Costa Rica on our fifth anniversary. We visited a hummingbird garden with more than fifty different types of hummingbirds. Frank went crazy taking pictures of them, and upon our return to Laguna, he'd insisted on buying several hummingbird feeders for our backyard. On weekends, we'd sit outside on the patio and listen to our hummingbird friends while we drank our coffee. Closing my eyes for a moment, I reached up to wipe away the tears that were burning in my eyes. Then I finished the rest of my lunch and trudged back inside.

At three-thirty, I was updating my notes on my last client when there was a loud knock on the door. "Come in," I said, as Zakiya tiptoed into my office. "So glad you made it." I smiled. "Have a seat." She was wearing a long-sleeved, red sweater with a short black skirt. Her hair was neatly pulled back behind her ears, revealing a pair of gold hoop earrings. She refused to meet my eyes.

"I was kind of forced into this," she muttered, taking the empty chair across from me.

"Well, I'm glad you're here. How were your classes today?"

"Same as always." She frowned, smoothing out the pleats on her skirt.

Sensing her resistance, I waited a few seconds to see if she would add something, only she didn't. I thought back to my first meeting with Tyrone and how long it had taken to gain his trust and confidence. It was always difficult to get teenagers to open up. "How's Tyrone?" I finally asked, hoping her close relationship with him would bring her closer to me.

"Same as last week," she shot, averting my eyes.

"You also have a younger brother, right?"

"You mean, Jerome? I can't stand him. Always in my face. He's not at all like Tyrone." There were glimpses of tenderness in her eyes now.

"What is Tyrone like?" I asked, watching her stretch out her long legs.

"He's always got my back."

"That's nice," I smiled. "I would've enjoyed having an older brother."

She drew in a quick breath, her eyes narrowing. "Don't you have any brothers?"

I hesitated for a moment before I answered her. "I had one, Andy, but he died very young."

Zakiya shot up. "Is there a bathroom in this place?"

The flushed look on her face made me realize I had screwed up by mentioning Andy. "Yes, right past the receptionist's desk," I replied, watching her race out the door. Disappointed in myself, I turned to gaze out the window, hoping I hadn't frightened her away. Just then, the door opened and Zakiya came back into the room and sat down. I breathed in a sigh of relief and moved back to my desk. I could tell that she had blotted her face with water from the tiny mascara stains in the corner of her eyes. She seemed more edgy, gazing nervously around the room.

"Tell me about your friends." I carefully asked, knowing that this was a safe topic. "Do you have a best friend?"

She pressed her lips into a scowl. "Peyton used to be my best friend, but she's been acting like a real bitch, so I dumped her."

"Did something happen between you?" I gently pried.

Zakiya shrugged. "No, she's just not my friend anymore."

Her words sounded bitter. It was clear that she didn't want to talk about Peyton, so I changed the subject.

"Tell me about your classes."

"They're all boring," she quipped, as she began to chip at the turquoise polish on her long slender fingers.

"There must be one class that you enjoy?"

She raised her head and shook it stubbornly, crossing her long smooth legs in front of her.

"What about clubs or sports?" I asked, unwilling to give in to her resistant attitude. "Are there any sports you like?"

"Is that why you wanted to see me, just to talk about things I like?" she asked in a sarcastic tone.

"Why do you think you're here?"

"How should I know?" she retorted. "You're the shrink, not me."

I could tell she was even more annoyed than before. It was obvious that she was trying to challenge me, but I wasn't about to give up.

After a long pause, Zakiya said, "You know very well my mom made me come." Then she reached for her backpack on the floor, announcing, "I have to go. I told Ty I'd meet him out front."

Following her to the door, I reached for her arm before she could leave. "Would you like to meet again next week?" I asked.

Zakiya hesitated for a moment, then shrugged her shoulders. "Maybe, I don't know," she mumbled, rushing out of my office as if the building were on fire.

Reaching for Frank's picture on my desk, I caressed it tenderly. "Thank you, Frank," I whispered, thinking back to all the times I'd come close to giving up on one of my teens, only to have Frank gently say, "These kids need you more than ever, Sandy, 'cause you understand them." *Yes, Frank, you were so right,* I admitted, brushing my fingers across the cool glass of the frame. I would do everything in my power to help Zakiya. After all, maybe I needed her as much as she needed me.

ELEVEN
Zakiya

The second I get on the bus, Manuel makes a joke about me ditching school. I've always hated riding the bus, but now it's worse since I have to put up with smart-ass remarks. When Micaela, a friend from MEChA, asks me to sit with her and Marissa, I say I have to finish my homework and I find an empty seat in the back. Then I pull out my science book from my backpack and pretend I'm reading. I could care less about Micaela and her stupid friends. I just want to be left alone.

I'm going up the steps toward the main quad when I come face to face with Mr. Gutiérrez, or Mr. G. as he's known around campus. He's one of the coolest people at this school, he never talks down to anyone and he's always straight up with us. I have no choice but to pause when he gives me one of his intense counselor stares, saying, "Zakiya, we missed you at our last MEChA meeting. How are you?"

Avoiding his eyes, I glance at the beaded choker that hangs around his neck. "Fine," I mumble. As I start to walk away, he promptly adds, "We have a MEChA meeting this Friday. Hope you can come."

"Can't make it," I say, shrugging, leaving him behind with a concerned look on his weathered Indian face. I don't know why I ever joined MEChA. Mr. G. is always trying to save the world with his Circles and all his indigenous talk. Not me. I couldn't care less about other people's problems anymore.

I'm approaching my locker when I feel someone tap me on the shoulder. It has to be Peyton. Annoyed, I whipped up an insult, but when I turn around, I'm surprised to see Becky.

"Hey, wanna have lunch at noon?" she asks.

"Yeah, sure," I nod, noticing she's wearing another long-sleeved blouse.

"Cool—I'll meet you over by the track."

As I turn around, I spot a couple of girls watching us. I recognize the short redhead who was with Peyton the other morning. "What the hell are you staring at?" I ask accusingly as I walk past them.

When I get to Performing Arts, I'm happy to find out that Dalana is absent. At least I won't have to put up with her crap today. The other good news is that we get to sit and watch the musical, *Chicago*. Mrs. Jessup has a bad cold, so she can barely talk. "It was choreographed by Bob Fosse," she explains in between coughs. "He came up with Jazz hands. And he was the one who coined the famous phrase, *Less is more*, but we'll talk about that later. For now, enjoy the movie."

It turns out that I couldn't stand the movie with all those fake people and phony dance moves. It's so stupid. Rich white people with their fancy top hats and the plastic smiles on their faces as if they didn't have a care in the world. *How can anyone be that happy? What about real life? What about people who suddenly die and leave you all alone?* The sound of the bell pulls me away from my thoughts and brings me right back to the moment.

As I leave Biology, I spot Carlos near the water fountain talking with a stupid freshman girl. They're both smiling and their arms are touching. When he sees me, Carlos nudges closer to her. What a jerk, he's gotta be desperate, hitting on a freshman.

After I drop off my books and grab my lunch from my locker, I make my way to the south end of campus behind the track field. Becky is already there sitting on the grass. She's drinking a soda and eating from a snack size bag of chips. "Is that all you're having?" I ask, sitting next to her.

Becky chuckles. "I need to lose a few so I can look like those skinny girls on Netflix. Who knows, I might want to be an actress one day."

"Get real," I tell her, taking out my sandwich. "I didn't see you in detention last week," I say cautiously. "Did you get suspended?"

"Yeah, but only for a day. My stepmom didn't care, but my dad was so pissed. How about you—did they give you hell?"

I hesitate for a moment, wondering if I should mention that my dad just died, but instead, I answer, "My momma did, she totally freaked."

"Tell me about it," Becky grumbles, tilting her head slightly. "I can't stand my stepmom, she's got my dad by the balls, if you know what I mean."

I give her a quiet nod, realizing that Becky's life is even worse than mine. At least my parents always stuck up for each other—even when one of them made a bad decision.

"You wanna hang out after school?" Becky asks, finishing the last of her soda.

"Wish I could, but I can't—my momma won't take her eyes off me. Tyrone either."

"Who's that?"

"My older brother—he's tries to act like my dad, all big and bad."

"Wish I had a big brother," Becky confesses, a wistful look on her freckled face. "I have two little brothers and I'm expected to be their babysitter all the time." Her face suddenly lighting up, Becky asks, "Wanna listen to Anville's new song?" As she reaches for her cell phone, I catch a glimpse of a tiny scar above her left wrist as the sounds of hip-hop fill the air. After we listen to a few more songs, we gather up our stuff and head back for fifth period.

∾ ∾ ∾

The second I walk through the door after school, Momma hollers out to me from the kitchen. I think about rushing upstairs, but she calls out my name even louder than before, so I have no choice but to obey. She's sitting at the kitchen table, her blue coffee mug next to her, and there are several unopened bills in front of her. "Tomorrow I start full time at the hospital, 8 a.m. to 4 p.m.," she explains. Tearing a sheet of paper from the notepad on the table, she waves at me. "Here's a list of the things you'll be responsible for as soon as you get home."

Cursing under my breath, I'm about to utter a complaint, when Jerome strolls into the kitchen. "Anything to drink, Ma?" he asks in that condescending tone he uses when he wants something.

A warm smile stretches across Momma's face. "Sure baby," she agrees, rising from the table to get him a soda from the refrigerator.

"Can't you get it yourself?" I sneer at Jerome, my lips quivering.

"Leave him be," Momma scolds me as he exits the kitchen, a smug look on his face.

Easing back into her chair, Momma begins to read the list of chores out loud for me. I'm tempted to ask her why Jerome can't do some of them, except I know it would be useless. If there's one thing I know for sure, it's that if Dad were here, he'd back me up. He wouldn't let Momma spoil the crap out of Jerome just because he's a guy.

Back upstairs in my room, I toss my backpack on the bed and collapse on my pillow, tears bursting out like a sudden rainstorm. After a while, I sit up, dry-eyed and reach for my backpack. Just then, I hear a light tap on the door and Tyrone comes into my room. "Were you crying, Zee?" he gently asks. "Are you all right?"

"I'm fine," I mumble while I open my Algebra book, hoping he'll quit asking questions.

Moving closer to the bed, he asks, "Need any help?"

"I'm fine," I snap, my words cold as ice. "Can't you see I'm trying to do my homework?"

"Sorry," he apologizes. "Just wanted to see how you were."

Turning to leave, he pauses to gaze at me with those piercing eyes that remind me of Dad. "You know, Zee, you're not the only one who misses him."

Tears flood my eyes after he shuts the door behind him. Feeling angry at Tyrone, at myself, I fling my Algebra book to the floor. I'm not being selfish, if that's what he thinks. If only Dad hadn't gone and died on us. If only he could've lived longer. Then things would be like before.

TWELVE
Zakiya

The next morning, Momma opens the door to my bedroom to announce she's leaving for her first full day of work at the hospital. Looking up at her, I say, "Wait, Momma. I don't feel good today." Then I release a few pathetic coughs, sounding as if I've got something stuck in my throat.

Momma opens the door wider, eyeing me shrewdly. "Zakiya, you better not be lying."

I shake my head, coughing a few more times. She comes over to my bedside and places her hand on my cheek. "You do feel a little warm. All right, I'll call the school, but I better not find out you left the house."

As soon as the door shuts behind her, I pull the covers back over my head. I'm drifting off to sleep when I hear Jerome's whiny voice. He's standing at the door, his headphones dangling from his big ears, "You might've fooled Momma, but I know you're faking it."

"Shut up!" I scream as he slams the door shut. Jerome used to be a sweet little boy. *Why did he ever have to grow up?* Unable to fall back asleep, I reach for my cell phone on the nightstand. I listen to music on YouTube for the next hour. When "4K" comes on, I feel a huge lump in my throat, remembering that this same song was playing on the radio the last time Dad gave me a ride home from school. He was so happy moving his shoulders as if he were dancing to it. When tears begin to slide down my face, I stop the video. Then I pull the blanket over my face, wishing I had forced myself to go to school.

After about an hour, my stomach starts to growl, so I climb out of bed and go into the bathroom. As I wash my face and brush my teeth, I stare at my reflection in the mirror. Dad always said I was beautiful like Momma. If he could only see me now. My eyes are red and my hair is sticking out all over the place. As I pat it down with my hand, I think about Carlos. I wonder if he still thinks I'm pretty. He's probably with that stupid freshman right now. I can picture him leaning into her, brushing his hand against her cheek. Screw him, at least I won't have to see him today.

It's peaceful downstairs without Momma's obnoxious voice ordering me around. After I pour myself a bowl of cereal, I take it into the living room, knowing that if Momma were here she'd have a hissy fit. I've only taken a few bites when my eyes fall on the framed picture of Momma and Dad on top of the television. It was taken the day they got married. Momma looks awfully young and pretty with her hair all smoothed back. She's wearing a white cotton dress while Dad is wearing a dark blue suit jacket. His handsome face has a huge smile on it that reminds me of one of those famous movie stars like Michael B. Jordan. Dad would always repeat the story of how he had to steal the bride that day, that he and Momma had to sneak away and get married at City Hall. Then he'd promptly turn to me and say, "But not you, Zee baby. The day you get married we're gonna have a big ole church wedding. I'll be the luckiest father to give such a beautiful bride away." Wiping away a single tear, I take my bowl back into the kitchen. Then I hurry upstairs and get dressed, grabbing my cell phone and backpack.

The city bus drops me off near the entrance to the cemetery. I walk around aimlessly for a few minutes until I find the section where Dad is buried. Unlike Momma who's been coming every Sunday, this is the first time I've been back since the funeral. When I come to Dad's grave, I fall onto my knees. "I'm right here, Dad," I whisper. "I need you so much. Ty needs you—we all need you." Covering my face with my hands, I begin to sob. After a very long minute, I sit up and gently caress his marble headstone. "Oh, Daddy, I miss you so much. Nothing is the same without you anymore. I hate music—I hate everything." I stand up and dry my tears, knowing that he's gone forever.

An hour later, I'm making my way across the playground when Mrs. Contreras, who is pushing her granddaughter in a stroller, asks me why I'm not in school today. Pretending I haven't heard her, I rush upstairs to our apartment and straight into my bedroom. I plop down on the edge of the bed, my eyes darting nervously around the room. When my eyes fall on the volleyball trophy I won last year, I go over and pick it up. I fling it into the wastebasket. I reach for the manicure set on my dresser and before I know it I'm rolling up my sleeves. I begin to poke at my arm, right next to the scab I have from last time, until small drops of blood trickle down my wrist. Breathing in, I feel the tightness in my chest relax. I poke at my arm several more times until a few more drops of blood appear. It's then that I close my eyes feeling as if I'm floating high above in the sky.

The sudden ringing of my cell phone brings me back to reality. Leaning back against my pillow, I glance at it. It's Momma, but I'm feeling so good that I let it ring. It continues to ring until I finally have no choice but to answer it.

"Zakiya, didn't you hear the phone ring?" Momma's voice bellows out. "Where were you?"

"Sorry, I was in the bathroom," I lie, hoping Mrs. Contreras doesn't rat on me to Momma.

"Are you feeling better?" she asks. The second I answer yes, she reminds me to make sure I've vacuumed the living room and dusted before she gets home from work.

"I'm sick—why can't Jerome do it?" I complain, but Momma ignores my question and says she has to go.

Later, I've just finished vacuuming when the doorbell rings. I'm stunned to find Dalana standing in the doorway. "What do *you* want?" I snap, eyeing her suspiciously.

"Aren't you gonna invite me in?" she asks, giving me one of her sweet, innocent smiles.

"Why would I do that?"

"I want to be friends again?" she insists. "I don't want us to be mad anymore."

Dalana's tender words and the sincere look on her face make me realize she really does care about me. In that moment, I'm not sure what to do, so I invite her inside.

"You weren't at school today," she cautiously remarks, while we both pick a spot on opposite ends of the couch.

"I have a cold," I explain, noticing that her eyes are scrutinizing every move I make. I can tell she doesn't believe a word I've said. When she suddenly looks at my arm, I stare at her, wondering if she might somehow know.

"Did you hurt yourself?"

"No," I bark at her. "Why would you ask me that?"

"There's blood on your shirt."

I look down at my sleeve and sure enough, blood has soaked through the band-aid and my shirt and left a stain the size of a quarter.

"Oh," I say, laughing nervously and tugging at my sleeve. "That's just ketchup, from lunch."

"I thought you were sick," she said.

"Sick people still have to eat," I say, shrugging. I can't bring myself to look her in the eyes to see if she believes me.

Pretending not to notice the lie, she says, "Peyton was asking about you."

"Screw her," I answer in a sarcastic tone, abruptly standing up and moving next to the vacuum cleaner. Bending down, I hastily begin to wind the cord back onto it. "I have a lot of work to do," I mutter. "Don't you have somewhere else to go?"

Her eyes narrowing, Dalana is on her feet. "Don't worry, I'm leaving," she defends herself. "I have to pick Mom up at work—just wanted to make sure you were okay."

"Why wouldn't I be?" I snap at her, but Dalana doesn't say a word.

At the door, she pauses to say, "I know how you feel, Zakiya. I miss my dad every single day."

"At least you still get to see him," I answer bitterly, closing the door in her face.

My eyes blurry, I'm filled with sadness and guilt. *Why did I have to treat Dalana like that? What's wrong with me?* She was only trying to be nice. Sometimes I wish I'd never been born.

THIRTEEN
Zakiya

On Friday, just as third period is about to end, I hear my name called on the intercom to report to the main office. Sitting behind me is nerdy Martin Paige and he whispers, "What'd you do now?"

"None of your business," I grumble, aware that all eyes are on me as I go up to Mr. B and he hands me a hall pass with his long bony fingers.

The minute I open the door, the student assistant tells me that Mr. Mellon wants to see me. Worried thoughts buzz through my head as I make my way to his office. His door is open and he promptly waves me inside, asking me to close the door behind me. His flat, dry voice warns me that it's something serious.

"Zakiya, this is a very delicate issue," he says, clearing his voice. "I called you in because a student has reported they suspect you've been cutting yourself."

There are knots forming in my stomach and my knees are wobbly. "That's a stupid lie—whoever said that is lying!" I argue, clenching my left hand in a fist.

Leaning forward in his chair, Mr. Mellon's voice grows soft. "Zakiya, we need to talk about this."

Panicky thoughts swirl in my head. "Somebody's been lying about me," I sneer at him. "They're just trying to get me in trouble."

"Are you sure about that?" he asks, his blue eyes, studying my face intently.

When I nod twice, he pleads with me one more time. "Zakiya, can we please talk about this?"

"There's nothing to talk about," I insist, avoiding his stare.

Mr. Mellon furrows his bushy eyebrows. "I've already called your mother. She should be here any moment."

I feel a shiver run through my body. "I only did it once," I blurt out just as Momma bursts through the door. Her cheeks are flushed and there's a frightened look in her eyes that I haven't seen since the time Dad left us.

Rushing over to me, she raises her voice in disgust. "What is wrong with you, girl? Have you lost your mind?" When Mr. Mellon asks her to sit down, Momma gazes at him intently. "Thank you kindly, Mr. Mellon, but Zakiya and I are going home right now."

Mr. Mellon politely rises to his feet as there's nothing he can do or say that will change Momma's mind. Like an obedient child, I follow Momma to the door. After he reminds Momma that she can call him anytime, Mr. Mellon turns to me, saying, "Zakiya, we'll talk soon."

Momma doesn't say a word to me until we're out of the main quad and in the parking lot. The second we're in the car, she orders me to roll up my sleeves. I know better than to mess with Momma, so I hastily roll up my left sleeve. At the sight of the small scabs on my arm, Momma turns away, letting her face fall onto the steering wheel. While I listen to her cry softly, I can't help but feel satisfied knowing I've hurt her, that she's not as strong and invincible as she pretends.

After a very long minute, Momma reaches for a Kleenex from her pocket and dries her tears. Then she quietly starts the car. She doesn't utter a single word to me as we drive back to the apartment. I'm gazing out the window in silence, when Dalana's face suddenly appears in my mind. She had to have been the one who ratted on me, the way she kept staring at my sleeve when she came to talk with me. Who else could it have been? I can feel the anger mounting inside of me. And here I thought she wanted to make up with me, be my friend again. I hate her—I'll never speak to her again.

The second Momma unlocks the front door and we step inside the living room, I turn toward the stairway only to find that Momma is right behind me. Like a crazy woman, she rushes after me upstairs to my bedroom. Then she frantically begins to search through my dresser, tossing my clothes on the floor. "What do you think you're doing?" I holler as she moves toward my nightstand. When she can't find what she's looking for, she reaches for the stapler on top of my dresser.

"Is this how you did it?" she asks, removing a few staples and holding them up to me.

"Stop it, Momma," I demand, only she's even more livid. She turns toward my closet and begins searching through my clothes throwing skirts on hangers and folded shirts and sweaters on to the floor. That's when the dam breaks wide open inside of me. I walk up behind her and shove her back, screaming, "Leave my things alone!"

It's at that exact moment when I hear Tyrone's familiar voice behind me. "What's going on here? Zee, stop it!" he hollers at me. In a daze, I quickly move to the side as he dashes toward Momma, putting his arms around her. "Are you okay, Momma?" he gently asks.

Momma gasps, releasing a long deep breath. "I'm all right, son," she mumbles, her eyes full of tears.

"Come on, Momma, we're going downstairs."

As they walk out of the room holding each other, Tyrone glares at me, raising his voice to say, "Zee, you and me are gonna talk."

After I frantically put everything back where it belongs, I stretch out on my bed, trying to calm down, only I can't. I'm plagued with guilt for attacking Momma like that. I've never done that before, but I couldn't help it. She made me so mad. She had no business barging into my room and going through my things. If Dad had been here, he would've stopped her. He wouldn't have let her treat me like that. I feel a sudden chill race up and down my spine as I sit in silence. *What if Momma tells Tyrone everything? What will Tyrone think of me then? She'll probably tell Jerome too. If only I could get away from here, but where would I go? Momma will ground me forever now.* I close my eyes as all these thoughts swirl in my head.

Moments later, Tyrone barges into my room without even knocking. His huge dark eyes look as if they are about to burst out of their sockets. "Momma told me what happened. Why'd you do it?" he asks bluntly. "Momma thinks you're trying to kill yourself. Is that true?"

I release a small, dry chuckle, shaking my head. "She's crazy—of course I'm not."

Sitting next to me on the edge of the bed, Tyrone places his hand over mine. "Zee, what can I do to help?" he asks, his voice low and tender. "You know I'm always here for you."

Bowing my head for a second, I'm suddenly afraid. *Why did Dad have to go and die? Why can't he be here to help me like all the times before?* I remember when I was in fifth grade and I fell off my bike and broke my arm. Dad put his arms around me and gently stroked my hair every night, telling me everything was going to be fine. "No one can help," I abruptly answer, our eyes meeting. "I just want to be left alone."

"I won't do that," Tyrone insists, his words firm as steel. "I'm going to call Ms. Martínez today."

"What for? It's Momma who needs a shrink. Not me."

"Zee, get real. It's not Momma's fault. You scared the hell out of her."

"Well, I hate her. I can't stand her."

Tyrone shakes his head, muttering something under his breath. "I have to get to class," he says. As he opens the door to leave, I can hear Momma's loud voice on the phone with Father Brown. Of course, Momma called him. She's probably filling his head with lies.

Later that night, I'm about to turn off my light when my phone rings. It's Tyrone. "I spoke with Ms. Martínez. She's agreed to see you tomorrow at eleven."

"On a Saturday? Are you crazy?" I answer, feeling a pinching sensation at the base of my neck. "I suppose you told her everything."

"Not all of it—but you have to go," Tyrone demands. "I'll drop you off on my way to the library."

As soon as we hang up, I reach for Dad's picture on my nightstand. "Oh, Daddy, what am I gonna do now?" I mutter out loud. I can hear his voice uttering those words that always used to soothe me, "I'm right here, baby." I close my eyes, imagining he's right by my side and suddenly I begin to feel better.

FOURTEEN
Dr. Martínez

The loud sounds of the garbage truck picking up the trash on our street woke me up, reminding me that it was Saturday morning. Frank's favorite day of the week. I could picture him seated at the kitchen table with his purple and gold Lakers mug drinking his milky cup of coffee while he scanned the morning news. Because he knew how much I loved to sleep in on weekends, he'd wait until it was almost nine o'clock before he began making breakfast. By the time I was out of bed, the house was filled with the aroma of hashbrowns and the greasy bacon he loved to eat, insisting it was good for his *pancita*. Afterward, we'd drive to one of the surrounding peaks for a long hike. When we returned home, Frank would pat his *pancita*, insisting it was getting smaller. Then he'd take a quick shower and leave for his office while I stayed behind to do the mundane household tasks.

"*Ni modo*," I whispered, as I glanced at the alarm clock. It was time to get ready for my eleven o'clock appointment with Zakiya. Over the years, I'd done my best to avoid going into my office on weekends, but when Tyrone called, he sounded desperate. In a frantic voice, he had described a terrible fight between Zakiya and his mother, asking if I could please see her today. The second I agreed, I heard a deep sigh on the other end of the line. Feeling grateful that I had something else to do besides lying here and thinking about Frank, I eagerly climbed out of bed and hurried into the shower.

I found Zakiya sitting on the front steps of my office building when I pulled into the driveway. Reaching for my small leather bag, I hurried out of the car. "You beat me," I smiled. "Hope you weren't waiting too long."

Shaking her head, she stood up, placing her phone in her tiny red handbag. She was wearing a pair of tight black jeans with a bright red sweater that made her look like a fashion model.

"Don't you have a life?" she snickered as I unlocked the front door and she followed me inside to my office. I was about to answer when Zakiya quickly apologized for her insensitive remark, "Sorry—I didn't mean it like that."

"Not to worry," I reassured her, though I couldn't help but wonder if Zakiya was right. Lately, that's exactly how I'd been feeling. No husband. No children. Just an empty life. Only I couldn't tell her that. As soon as we were both seated, I waited patiently for her to begin talking while I watched her fidget with the beaded bracelet on her wrist. After a few seconds, she tilted her chin up at me and said, "I suppose Tyrone told you I shoved my mom."

"He mentioned you had a bad fight, but he didn't tell me that part," I explained. I suddenly understood Tyrone's anxiety. Just like in the past when he'd dropped out of school to help Mrs. Cameron, here he was again feeling responsible for protecting and providing for his family.

Uncrossing her long legs and fidgeting in her seat, Zakiya sneered, "Momma had it coming to her."

"What makes you say that?" I asked.

Zakiya squirmed in her chair, her dark eyes blazing like hot coals. "I can't stand Momma. She's such a bitch. I wish I could get away from her, move to Oakland with my aunt."

Putting her head down, her body suddenly went limp as she began to cry. I quickly moved to her side and handed her several tissues and held her arm gently until her tears subsided. "I wish Dad were here," she sniffled. "I hate Momma so much."

As I went back to my desk chair, I gently pried, "Can you tell me what started the fight?"

There was a long moment of silence as she rubbed her hands nervously until she finally lifted her head, the words spilling out of her mouth. "Momma found out I cut myself. Big mouth Dalana told the counselor and he called Momma. And now she won't leave me alone. She's watching me all the time. She even comes into my room at night when I'm asleep." Clenching her teeth, Zakiya went on, "And the worst part is that she insists on checking my arms and wrists. I can't stand it. She won't leave me alone, that's why I hit her. I didn't mean to, but she went crazy after Mr. Mellon told her. She tore my room apart and searched through my clothes. That's when I pushed her." She looked away then, tears filling her eyes.

I breathed in slowly, taking a few moments to collect my thoughts. I hadn't expected this sudden revelation, but it all made sense now—Tyrone's fear, Mrs. Cameron's reaction. It was not uncommon for parents to react with anger and fear when they found out their children were hurting themselves. "Zakiya," I slowly began. "It's extremely hard on parents when they find out their son or daughter is self-injuring."

"But I only did it twice," she defended herself. "If Dad were here, he'd stick up for me."

"It sounds like you're missing him a lot," I consoled her, knowing exactly how she was feeling. I wished Frank were still here to lean on, especially when things went wrong. The other night when the light had gone out in the garage, I found myself wishing he were still here as I nervously climbed the ladder to replace the light bulb.

Wiping away a tear that rolled down her cheek, Zakiya explained. "Dad was the only one I could talk to—he understood me. I could tell him anything and he wouldn't get pissed off like Momma."

Leaning forward in my chair, I asked, "And do you think injuring yourself is the answer?" I waited patiently while she shifted her weight in her seat. It was important that she recognize the connection between her emotional pain over her father's sudden death and her self-injury.

"I only did it twice," she argued. "It's not like I do it all the time. Besides, my friend Becky does it and she's cool."

"Is that why you did it—to feel cool?" I asked.

"It made me feel good, that's why," Zakiya said. "Momma's been such a bitch since Dad died."

"Zakiya," I asked, "do you think there might be other ways to feel better?"

Shuffling her feet, she looked up at me. "Maybe. I don't know."

"What if you and I were to work together to find other solutions?"

Zakiya hesitated for a moment or two, then mumbled, "Yeah, I guess so."

"Good," I nodded, feeling a wave of confidence filter through my body. "But there's one more thing. I'd also like to talk with your mother about what happened, if that's okay with you."

Her body stiffened and her voice was suddenly shrill. "I knew you'd side with Momma—I told Tyrone you'd stick up for her."

"Zakiya, I'm not siding with anyone," I carefully explained. "This is a serious issue that involves the entire family. It's very important for me to talk with your mother, but please understand anything you and I talk about is strictly confidential. What we discuss always stays in this room."

The room filled with silence while she began to fuss with her bracelet again. After a minute or two, she let out a long deep sigh. "Okay, go ahead, but I'm warning you— Momma won't listen to anyone."

"Let me worry about that," I reassured her with a grin. "And thank you for trusting me."

Just then, her phone beeped. Reaching for it in her purse, she glanced at the text message. "It's Tyrone," she stated, standing up. "He's outside waiting for me." Then she dashed out the door before I could ask her about our next appointment.

Smiling to myself, I looked at Frank's photograph on my desk. "You always knew how much I loved helping people. Didn't you, Frank?" I whispered, realizing I felt more alive than I'd felt in months. Turning to gaze out the window, I noticed that the fog had lifted and the sun was peeking through the clouds. "Maybe this is a good day for a short hike. What do you think, Frank?" I asked him, gathering up my belongings to take a walk.

FIFTEEN
Dr. Martínez

Mrs. Cameron had agreed to meet with me after Sunday mass at St. Paul's, the small parish she attended in the nearby city of Al Mar. At first, she was hesitant, saying it was Zakiya that needed my help, not her, but I finally convinced her we needed to talk. As I pulled off the freeway and drove into Al Mar, I felt a slight shiver run through my body. Frank used to love going to the five-screen movie theater in Al Mar where he would stuff his *pancita* with popcorn and nachos piled high with jalapeños, his favorite snack. Frank would often tease that he should've been born a Mexican because he loved spicy food. Forcing myself back to the moment, I continued driving until I finally arrived at the church.

As I parked the car and made my way to the front, I was once again filled with remorse. If only Frank and I had attended church more often, maybe then he wouldn't have taken his life. Blinking back the tears, I spotted Father Brown standing at the entrance. Dressed in his priest vestments, he was shaking hands with the last of his parishioners. The moment he saw me, he greeted me with a smile. "Nice to see you again, Dr. Martínez. Martha's still inside. Would you like for me to get her?"

I was about to respond when Mrs. Cameron walked out of the church. She was wearing a modest black dress and her thick black hair was slicked back, making her look years younger.

"Dr. Martínez, glad you found it," she greeted me in a dry tone of voice.

"It was easy to find," I answered. Father Brown edged closer to our side. Pointing his long slender finger toward the area next to the main office, he explained, "I told Martha you can use one of our meeting rooms. This is where we often have dinners for special events. You'll have all the privacy you need."

I followed Mrs. Cameron through the courtyard to the small building next to the office. Once we were inside the dimly lit room, I pointed to two chairs near the window where the light filtered in, brightening the room. It was sparsely furnished, except for a long rectangular table and chairs and a small wooden cabinet against the wall. There were two large statues of the Virgin Mary and one of St. Jude at both ends of the room.

I could tell that Mrs. Cameron was nervous by the way she kept folding and unfolding the parish bulletin in her hands. I needed to choose my words carefully so that I wouldn't frighten her away. "Thank you for agreeing to see me today," I began.

Her eyes opening wide, she abruptly said, "Jerry spoiled Zakiya rotten ever since she was a baby. I know she's just doing it to get attention."

I cringed at the harsh tone of her words. Her reasoning sounded all too familiar. When parents find out their children are self-injuring, they often insist they are doing it to get attention. It is a false assumption, but she didn't know that. "Mrs. Cameron," I carefully explained. "Cutting is often a method many teens use when they don't know how to cope with their emotional pain."

Waving her folded bulletin wildly in the air, Mrs. Cameron's words were like bolts of lightning. "What's Zakiya got to worry about? Not a darn thing. It's me who has to pay the bills and take care of the household now that Jerry's gone."

Her almond-shaped eyes were bright with anger. It was obvious she felt overwhelmed with her unexpected new role as a single parent. Over the years, I'd often counselled single mothers in the same financial and emotional desperation. I reached out to pat her hand, but she quickly jerked it away. I bit the inside of my bottom lip. This was going to be harder than I imagined.

"I understand how you must be feeling with Mr. Cameron's sudden death, but it's important to understand that the death of a loved one affects the entire family. Zakiya is also hurting deeply from her father's unexpected death. And self-injury is her way of coping with her emotions."

"What about me?" Mrs. Cameron lashed out. "What about Tyrone, Jerome, don't you think we're hurting too?"

Before I could reply, she bowed her head slightly as the tears began to surface. After a few seconds, she gazed up at me, "Dr. Martínez," she whimpered. "I don't know what to do. I was so afraid when I found out she cut herself. Maybe

I acted mean and crazy, but I was so afraid she'd kill her-self, that she'd die like Jerry. That's why I won't let her out of my sight." Her voice faltered for a second. "Jerry always used to say Zakiya was strong, fearless." When she began to cry more, I reached out to place my arm around her shoulder. I could feel her intense fear.

Wiping away the last of her tears with her bright blue handkerchief, Mrs. Cameron looked up at me. "I always thought it was white girls that cut themselves and that black girls didn't do that."

I resisted the urge to smile, but now was not the time to talk about that false belief. "Mrs. Cameron, I'd like to meet with you and Zakiya in my office sometime next week. It's imperative that both of you talk about your feelings with each other."

Her dark eyes narrowed in fear. "I don't think that's a good idea. Zakiya despises me. I'm sure you know she shoved me."

I breathed in slowly, knowing how difficult it was to convince parents to agree to a session with their children. "Cutting is very frightening for parents. They often react with their own anger and fear. But we all need to work together if we want to help Zakiya. This is why we all need to talk. It's not about blaming anyone. Parental involve-ment is extremely important, even if we only meet a few times. So what do you say?"

She released an exasperated sigh. "I work every day until four, then by the time I finish with dinner it's late."

"That's not a problem. My schedule is flexible—I can see you anytime that works for you."

"She won't listen," Mrs. Cameron repeated in a shrill voice. "Zakiya hates me more than ever." Then, glancing at her wristwatch, she said, "I have to go. Zakiya and Tyrone will be back any minute. I can't leave her alone and Tyrone's gotta leave for school."

"Will you please think about it?" I gently pried as she rose to her feet.

Mrs. Cameron reluctantly nodded, "All right—I'll do anything to help my daughter." Then, clutching her black purse tightly, she left the room.

I waited for a minute while I massaged the tension in the back of my neck before I went outside. As I was going through the small courtyard, I heard someone call out my name. It was Father Brown. He was coming out of the Main office, only now he was dressed in a pair of brown slacks and a cotton shirt. "How did it go, Dr. Martínez?" he asked, walking up to my side.

"It went well, I hope."

"If there's anything I know about Martha, it's that she's stubborn as a mule," he said, smiling. "But don't you worry, I'll talk with her. I have an idea that might help."

"How long have you known the family?" I asked, wondering what he had in mind. It was obvious that Mrs. Cameron had complete confidence in him.

"Why don't we sit for a minute," he asked, pointing to a small bench. As we sat down, I breathed in the sweet scent coming from the red and yellow rosebushes that lined the courtyard.

"I've been with this parish for almost ten years. That's when I first met Mr. and Mrs. Cameron. Jerry was a fine man."

"You must be the only African American Catholic priest in this area," I bluntly stated.

Father Brown chuckled, his face glistening like a bronze statue. "You're right about that and I'm probably the first one from New Orleans too."

"Is that where you're from?" I asked, relieved he hadn't been offended by my remark. "I've never been to New Orleans but my husband and I always talked about taking a trip there for Mardi Gras." I felt a sudden piercing in my heart. Looking down at my feet, I pretended to fuss with the buckle on my sandals.

"Martha told me about your loss," he said, patting me gently on the shoulder. "I'm very sorry. How are you getting by?"

Unable to bear the look of pity in his black eyes, I abruptly stood up. The last thing I needed was a sermon about the afterlife, about God's mercy and goodness. "I'm better, thank you. I need to get on the freeway before the traffic gets bad."

Nodding, Father Brown said, "Remember, Dr. Martínez, if you need to talk about anything, just call the main office and they'll give you my direct line."

When I pulled out of the parking lot, Father Brown was still standing in the courtyard. As I waved back at him, I felt pangs of guilt, wondering if I myself was trying to avoid reality just like Mrs. Cameron and Zakiya.

SIXTEEN
Zakiya

On Monday, I'm in my first period English class when Mr. Mellon calls me into his office. I'm actually glad because Mrs. Harrison is revising our essays and she's a beast when it comes to grammatical errors. I absolutely hate grammar, but I love studying poetry—it has rhythm like dance movements. It's not stiff and boring like grammar.

The moment I sit down, Mr. Mellon begins, "I spoke with your mother this morning and she reassured me that you've started meeting with Dr. Martínez, a local psychologist. How is that going?"

"Fine," I answer, staring at his dull face. I imagine the lies Momma told him so he would get off her back and she would appear saintly.

"And how are you doing in all your classes?"

When I repeat the same one-word answer, Mr. Mellon gets the message. I have nothing to say to him or Momma. Straightening out his stupid bow tie that makes him look like a clown, he reminds me that he's here if I ever want to talk about anything. I almost laugh, but don't. Mr. Mellon and I have nothing to talk about. Has he forgotten that he's white and I'm black and that we come from two different worlds.

Later, I'm in the locker room changing into my yoga pants when I spot Dalana talking with a couple of girls. I walk straight up to her and give her a light push on her left shoulder. There is a stunned look on her face as her two friends quickly hurry away.

"Why'd you do that?" Dalana asks, her eyes brimming with tears.

"You know why—for being a stupid loud-mouth."

"That's not true," she says, her cheeks bright red. "I told Mr. Mellon because I care about you, that's why."

"Why don't you stop trying to be Miss Nicest Black Girl for a change. Why don't you focus on your stupid Prison Dad and stay out of my life!"

"Bitch," she hollers after me as I head into the gym.

While we do our warm-up, Dalana makes a point of staying on the opposite end of the gym. I know that I've hurt her badly because if anyone ever dared to say one bad word about my dad, I'd punch the hell out of them.

After third period, I'm leaving the science building when I run into Peyton. "Wait a minute." She smiles. "Do you want to have lunch with me today?"

The look of pity on her face warns me that Dalana has told her everything. Raising my voice, I snicker. "I wouldn't be caught dead with you or Dalana." Then I swiftly head toward my locker.

By lunchtime, I'm so pissed off that I ignore the rumbling in my stomach. I walk around and around the empty baseball field filled with angry thoughts about Peyton and Dalana. When I've finally calmed down, I find an empty spot behind the bleachers where I can avoid all the fake smiles and conversations going on around me. I stay there thinking about my messed-up life and friends until lunch period finally ends.

I'm racing into Spanish class trying to beat the bell, when I accidentally bump elbows with Carlos, who is also rushing through the doorway.

"Sorry," he mumbles, avoiding my eyes as we hurry and take our seats. While Mr. Villamil gives a brief introduction to the video we'll be watching about Ecuador, I wonder if Carlos is still with that stuck-up freshman girl. When I find myself secretly hoping they broke up, I have to remind myself that *I* was the one who rejected him. As soon as class ends, I'm the first one out the door.

Back at the apartment, I've just shut the door behind me, when the doorbell rings two times in a row. I decide to ignore it, thinking it might be Jerome pretending he forgot his keys just to piss me off. When it rings again, I fling the door open only to find Father Brown standing in the doorway. "Momma's not home yet," I stammer.

"It's you I wanted to see—can I come in?" he asks, a twinkle in his eyes.

I'm tempted to shut the door in his face, but the white collar under his jacket is very intimidating. I politely invite him into the living room. I wouldn't want to go to hell for saying *no* to a priest. Besides, Dad admired Father Brown a lot. I once heard him tell Momma that Father Brown's sermons were almost as powerful as Dr. King's.

Once we're both seated on the couch, Father Brown says, "Young lady, I have an exciting proposition for you. I know how much you love to dance. Jerry was always saying you wanted to be a dancer, that you loved music, so I thought of you right away."

Feeling a sudden tightening in my heart, I gaze up at Father Brown. It's true—Dad always believed in me when I told him I wanted to be a hip-hop dancer. But why is it that Father Brown is suddenly so concerned about me and my dreams? I wouldn't doubt it if Momma told him I was trying to kill myself.

"One of our parishioners, Marivel Lozano, is the director of Bravo Dance Studio. It's a small after-school program for low-income kids whose parents work in the fields. It's been very successful giving kids the opportunity to take free dance classes and give performances throughout the area. Marivel could certainly use some help with her dance classes. And you'd be a wonderful role model for these kids. What do you say? Would you like to be her assistant?"

I can feel my heart fluttering with excitement. It would be so cool to be in a real dance studio, but what if Momma put him up to this? And why should I care about anyone else? My life is all screwed up—I can barely take care of myself. It's hard enough keeping Momma off my back. "I can't do it," I say. "I have too much homework every night."

Father Brown leans forward, his eyes on me like a laser beam. "It would only have to be on weekends, that way it wouldn't interfere with your school work."

"I wouldn't have a way to get there either," I say emphatically, glancing down at his shiny black shoes.

He's about to utter another convincing statement when the door suddenly opens and Momma walks into the living room.

"Father Brown, what a nice surprise," she says, smiling. Her face is drawn and her body seems to weigh on her like a pile of bricks.

"Hello, Martha," he says, standing up while Momma takes off her bright blue winter coat. After they hug briefly, he explains, "This time it was Zakiya I came to see. How was work today?"

"A busy one. I hope you can stay for dinner?"

Father Brown gives her a radiant smile. "Just so happens I'm free until evening Mass."

When Momma begins telling Father Brown about the grouchy lady in housekeeping who suddenly quit today, I exit the room before she even notices. In my bedroom, I kick off my shoes and plop down on the bed with my backpack. I take out my phone and search Bravo Dance Studio. After I check out the website and look at the pictures with the students, I try to do my science homework, only I can't concentrate. All I can think about is being in a real dance studio.

Later, I get a text message from Momma telling me it's time to eat, that Jerome is spending the night at a friend's and Tyrone has a late class. When I walk into the kitchen, Father Brown is seated in Dad's chair at the head of the table. I want to order him to move, but I suck it up, taking the empty seat across from him. As I serve myself some spaghetti, Father Brown says, "Best spaghetti I ever had." Momma's face lights up as she passes me the salad.

In between mouthfuls, Father Brown brings up the dance studio again. "I hope you don't mind that I told your mother about it. She thinks it's a very good idea, that your father would be proud of you."

Out of the corner of my eye, I can see the smirk on Momma's face. What do I care what she thinks? After all, it's my life, not hers.

"Jerry used to love to sing in church," Momma says, her words soft as silk.

Reaching out to pat Momma on the hand, Father Brown says, "I can still see him sitting in the front pew belting out the lyrics to 'Bringing in the Sheaves.'"

"Father Brown," I suddenly speak up, "remember the time Dad screwed up and he started to sing the wrong song? Everyone was staring at him, but Dad didn't care, he kept right on singing until Momma elbowed him."

I let out a few chuckles as Father Brown begins to laugh boisterously. All of a sudden, Momma rises to her feet and begins to gather up the dinner plates. I become even more irritated when she turns on the disposal. How can Momma act so rude when we have company? Sensing my anger, Father Brown leans forward to whisper, "Your Momma's just trying to be strong—Jerry was the love of her life. Be patient with her. You both need each other's help now more than ever."

I nod quietly as Momma comes back to the table to ask Father Brown if he'd like another cup of coffee. Rising from the table, he shakes his head and tells her, "I'll have to take a rain check, Martha. Don't want to be late to give Mass tonight." Then Father Brown turns to me, saying, "I can't wait to see you at the dance studio."

After I've done the dishes, I'm headed toward the stairway when the door is flung open and Tyrone appears inside the living room. "Hey, Zee, I saw Father Brown leaving. What was that all about?" he asks.

"He had dinner with us." Hesitating for a moment, I tell him all about Father Brown's visit, adding, "He wants me to help out at this dance studio near his church."

"You should do it, Zee," Tyrone insists. "I can take you to check it out this weekend if you want."

"I'll think about it," I answer just as Momma comes into the living room to interrupt our private conversation. "Son, you must be starved," she says sweetly. "I saved a plate for you on the counter."

Then she gives me a hard stare. "Girl, don't just stand there," she orders me. "The floor needs to be swept."

SEVENTEEN
Zakiya

I can't stop thinking about the dance studio all week until Tyrone convinces me to go see it with him on Saturday. It's hard to say no to him because he reminds me so much of Dad. When I look at him, it's as if I'm gazing at the same strong jaw, the same kind eyes. I want to curl up in his arms and never let go. I'm so afraid he'll disappear from my life like Dad. Sometimes I catch Jerome staring at us with jealousy in his eyes. I never thought about it before, but maybe Tyrone reminds him of Dad too.

"Let's stop at In-N-Out on the way home," Tyrone says as we pull into Al Mar.

"I don't want to," I say sharply. The last time we went there we were with Dad. We were on our way home from the beach and we cheered and clapped when Dad took the exit to the restaurant. I can still hear him raving to Momma, "These here are the best burgers and fries in the world." Surprisingly, she agreed with him while we wolfed down our burgers and shakes. *How could Tyrone even think of going there without Dad?*

His voice sounding wistful, Tyrone says, "Zee, it might help, you know. I think Dad would like knowing we haven't forgotten all the things he liked to do with us."

"Do you think so?" I ask, my thoughts whirling. I remember the day in our Spanish class when Mr. Villamil showed a film about Day of the Dead. It showed how in Mexico, since pre-Columbian times, death was celebrated as a part of life. Then it flashed to the present day, showing families making altars for their loved ones, even taking food to their graves because they believe their spirits are always near. I never thought about it until now, but maybe Dad would like it if we went to In-N-Out.

We continue through the downtown streets of Al Mar until we arrive at the small red-brick building with the large sign on the front window that reads Bravo Dance Studio. "Looks cool," Tyrone says, parking across the street.

I can feel my knees wobble as we make our way to the dance studio. The moment we step inside we are greeted by the sounds of Mariachi music and a room decorated with Mexican art. The walls, which are painted a bright red and green, are adorned with an assortment of wooden paintings and colorful sarapes. My eyes rest on the Mexican flag just like the one Mr. Villamil has in our classroom.

"Can I help you?" asks the sandy-haired woman behind the desk.

"We came to visit the dance studio," Tyrone politely explains while I remain mute. "We were told to ask for the director."

Smiling, she rises to her feet. "I'm Rosa, the receptionist. Follow me, Marivel is in the back with the girls."

We follow Rosa through a narrow hallway into a large room where the Mariachi music is even louder. A group of girls dressed in long Mexican dresses are spread out on the dance floor. "That's her," Rosa states, pointing to the short brown woman at the front of the small stage. "Now, I need to get back to the front desk."

The second Marivel spots us, she comes over to our side.

Tyrone is the first one to speak. Shaking her plump hand, he explains, "I'm Tyrone and this is my sister, Zakiya. Father Brown gave us your address."

"Oh, yes," she grins, revealing two large dimples. "So glad you're here." Then she turns toward me. "Zakiya, I could sure use your help with the girls. Father Brown said you love music and dance."

"Yes, I do," I reply timidly, as Marivel signals for the music to stop. Then, instructing the girls to move closer, she announces. "This is Zakiya. She's thinking of becoming our new assistant." I can feel their eyes on me while she introduces each of the girls from youngest to oldest.

When Tyrone gives me a slight nudge, I mumble hello, feeling slightly embarrassed to find myself the center of attention. After she thanks them, Marivel motions for the music to start again. Then she instructs the tallest girl to take over as the instructor. We follow Marivel back to the reception area where she takes us across the room to a large whiteboard. "This is our weekly schedule. As you can see, we don't just teach Ballet Folklórico. Gazing directly at me, she adds, "Zakiya, Father Brown said you liked hip-hop, is that right?"

Once more, Tyrone gives me a slight jab so that I can speak up. "Yes, that's my favorite, but in my Performing Arts class we're learning all types of dance."

"The girls love my hip-hop dance class. If you're willing to help me with that one, I can move the schedule around for whatever days you can come."

This time I'm really annoyed when Tyrone answers for me. "Zakiya's free on Saturdays."

Marivel grins when I flash a warning look at Tyrone. "That's perfect. Here's my phone number," she says, handing me her card. "I really hope you can make it. I know the girls would really like you."

"Thanks," I answer, just as one of the girls hollers out into the hallway that they need help with the next dance.

"Sorry, I have to go," Marivel apologizes. "But come back anytime you want."

As we go back outside to the car, I'm about to scold Tyrone for butting into my business when he asks, "So what do you think, Zee?"

I hesitate for a moment, then say, "It's a cool place—the girls are cute."

"Like I said, I can give you a ride on Saturdays."

"I told you I'd think about it," I snap back. I know Tyrone is just trying to be sweet, but I don't like it when I'm being pressured.

We're driving back toward the freeway when Tyrone asks, "So what do you say—In-N-Out?"

"Why not?" I nod, knowing Tyrone is right. This would make Dad very happy.

After he drops me off at the apartment, I find Momma on the couch doing one of her boring crossword puzzles. Looking up at me, she asks, "Isn't Tyrone coming in?"

"He had to go to the library."

"How was the dance studio?"

"Fine," I answer, turning toward the stairway, but before I can leave, Momma is at my side.

"Wait, Zakiya, we need to talk."

"Oh, yeah, about what?" I ask, standing there awkwardly.

Momma's eyes narrow. "I wanted to talk with you the other night, but Father Brown was here. I spoke with Dr. Martínez. She wants us both to meet with her. I told her I would do it."

"That was smart," I answer sarcastically, realizing I never once thought Momma would agree with Ms. Martínez's screwed up idea.

"Zakiya," Momma says, her voice barely a whisper. "I don't want you to hurt yourself. Don't you know I love you as much as your father did?"

"Liar!" I shout back accusingly, only this time Momma backs off as I race to my bedroom.

∽ ∽ ∽

Later that evening, I'm going downstairs to the kitchen for a glass of water, when I hear muffled sobs coming from Momma's bedroom. I feel a sudden tightening in my chest and I'm filled with an overwhelming guilt. Could Father Brown have been right about Momma? Maybe she does miss Dad as much as I do. Maybe he was her one true love just like in Romeo and Juliet.

EIGHTEEN
Dr. Martínez

When my three o'clock appointment ended fifteen minutes early, I breathed a sigh of relief. Leaning back in my desk chair, I closed my eyes for a moment. It had been a very busy Thursday with no cancellations. I'd barely had time to eat lunch before my next client arrived. I used to complain endlessly about days like these to Sonia, but with Frank's death, keeping so damn busy made it easier to bear the emptiness. Gazing at Frank's photograph, I couldn't help but think of all the times Frank supported me despite those endless hours of work. My thoughts drifted to the hours I'd spent with Juanita and Sam Turner that terrible year, all those disgusting school board meetings. The day we'd received the news that Juanita was finally reinstated back in school, Frank pulled me into his arms, whispering, "That's why I love you so much, Sandy, because you care about those who need help the most."

As I reached up to wipe away a tear, there were several light knocks on the door. I found Mrs. Cameron and Zakiya standing in the doorway. "Nice to see you both—please come in." I smiled, feeling confident that I'd been able to convince Mrs. Cameron of how important it was for her and Zakiya to meet with me. I could feel the negative energy between them as they followed me to my desk. It was always extremely difficult for both parents and teens to talk openly while they were both in the same room. Most of the time it ends up in a screaming match, with one of them angrily leaving the room. I certainly hoped it wouldn't be like that today.

As Zakiya took the chair next to my desk, I complimented her on the maroon sweater she was wearing, hoping to ease the tension. When she mumbled a curt thank you, Mrs. Cameron frowned. She looked at me and said, "It's a little too tight if you ask me."

"No one's asking you," Zakiya hissed.

"Hush your mouth, girl!"

Zakiya focused her gaze on me and said, "I don't understand why we both had to come."

I was about to respond, when Mrs. Cameron snapped at her. "Don't get on your high horse—Dr. Martínez knows exactly what she's doing."

Raising my voice slightly before the tension in the room could escalate, I carefully explained, "It's very important for me to meet with both the parents and their teens to ensure we're all working together, that we have the same goals and expectations." I paused to reach for several business cards on my desk, handing one to each of them. "Now both of you have my number. I want you to know that if you need to talk, you can call me on my cell anytime, any hour of the day."

"Even if it's three in the morning?" Zakiya asked, her big eyes widening.

"Yes."

"That's awfully kind of you," Mrs. Cameron said, slipping the card into her black purse.

"The first thing I'd like to do today is to review my policy of confidentiality."

"What's all of that?" Mrs. Cameron asked, a puzzled look on her face.

"I want both you and Zakiya to know that whatever we talk about in this room, stays in this room. Also, Mrs. Cameron, when I meet individually with Zakiya or with you, that will also be kept confidential."

Mrs. Cameron tilted her head, arching her left eyebrow. "Then how in Jesus' name am I supposed to know if Zakiya's trying to hurt herself again?"

"That's none of your business," Zakiya fired back.

"Mrs. Cameron," I began gently. "I know that as a parent you would want to know if your daughter were hurting herself and I can reassure you, under those circumstances, I would not hesitate in contacting you. But only if it had to do with your child's safety."

I turned back to Zakiya, who had a smug look on her face. I calmly continued, "Above all, I want your mother to know that she can speak with me at any time she wishes about any concerns that she may have."

I could see the relief filter into Mrs. Cameron's dark brown eyes. "And Zakiya, the second thing I want to clarify in your mom's presence today is the absolute commitment you and I have made to address the emotions that led you to self-injure. It's very important for you to take this commitment as seriously as I do so that we can find solutions together."

Zakiya shifted in her chair. "Yes, I agree," she began, "but I don't want Momma around. It's bad enough she watches every move I make."

"It's because I love you, that's why," Mrs. Cameron insisted, her eyes watery. "I don't want you to hurt yourself anymore."

"That's a lie," Zakiya quipped. "The only ones you love are Ty and Jerome."

Frank's mother suddenly came into my thoughts. I knew she still blamed me for his death. It was easier to blame someone else than to look deep inside, to examine your own feelings. Zakiya was doing the exact same thing. She was blaming her mother.

Shaking her head fiercely, Mrs. Cameron attempted to defend herself while Zakiya covered her ears with her hands.

"I'm on your side, Zakiya—why won't you believe me?" Mrs. Cameron explained in a weary voice. "That's why I agreed with Father Brown the other night—I support you one hundred percent about the dance studio."

"What dance studio?" I eagerly asked.

Zakiya's eyes were shining as Mrs. Cameron began to recount the entire evening of Father Brown's unexpected visit and his surprising offer to Zakiya, that she become an assistant at Bravo Dance Studio.

Zakiya made a face. "See what I mean—she never lets me talk."

"It sounds like a wonderful opportunity," I said, ignoring her remark. "I hope you seriously think about it."

"Yeah, I guess," she shrugged, trying to act nonchalant, but the light in her eyes told me something different.

There was another moment of silence until Mrs. Cameron raised her head to say, "Dr. Martínez, there was something else I wanted to ask you."

Zakiya's head jerked up as if she were preparing for another round of criticism from her mother.

"I was wondering about Jerome," she stated in a clear, calm voice. "I haven't told him anything at all, but I know he suspects something. He's the only one in the family who doesn't know what's been happening. He's only in junior high, so I'm not sure what to do."

"Jerome's a little creep and it's none of his business," Zakiya protested, her words bitter and sharp.

I quickly intervened. "It's very important that the entire family knows what's been going on, especially Jerome. Often parents attempt to keep things secret from their other children, thinking it's a way of protecting them. But it often ends up creating more problems. Kids are very smart, they know and feel when something has changed in the family dynamics. Keeping this from him may cause him even more worry and anxiety."

Nodding, Mrs. Cameron suggested, "When Jerry was alive, he always called a family meeting when there was a problem."

There was anger in Zakiya's eyes as she lashed out at her mother. "That's stupid—you're just trying to act like Dad! You'll never be like him!"

When Mrs. Cameron pursed her lips, I knew she was trying to restrain herself. It was always difficult for parents to manage their own anger and guilty feelings when their teenagers were insensitive.

"I think that's a very good idea," I complimented Mrs. Cameron. "If it's something that worked in the past, I would suggest trying it again."

"It won't work and I won't do it," Zakiya said, her words loud and threatening.

In that moment, I decided it was best not to pursue this any further, enough had been said for today. I would talk about this with Zakiya in our next session. "Why don't we stop here?" I announced. "But do remember what I said, feel free to call me any time one of you needs to talk. And Zakiya, do call me so we can schedule another session."

As I closed the door behind them, I took a long deep breath, attempting to release all the tension I'd gathered from Zakiya and Mrs. Cameron. This was going to be harder than I thought. If only Frank were here to lean on. He could always find a way to calm my doubts and fears, reminding me that everything would work out, only now, I couldn't.

NINETEEN
Zakiya

When Saturday morning finally arrives, I'm so hyped about going to the dance studio that I wake up super early. I've always dreamed of performing in a real dance studio. Aunt Marilyn once told me that when I was little I was always pretending to be a contestant on *Dancing with the Stars*. Dad would correct her, saying I learned to dance from him because from the time I was born he'd pick me up in his arms and we'd sail around the room. If only Dad were here now. Maybe it's like Tyrone said, he's watching everything we do from heaven.

After I shower, I tiptoe downstairs so I won't wake anyone up, but Momma is already in the kitchen. She's having her coffee while she makes breakfast. The smell of bacon reminds me of all those weekends I'd find Dad at the table happily stuffing himself with Momma's greasy bacon and fried potatoes. "Zee, your momma should've been a cook," he'd say, insisting he'd married Momma because of her cooking. Momma's face would brighten and she'd let out one of her stupid little laughs.

"Tyrone said he'd be here by nine to pick you up. How about some bacon and eggs?" she asks, glancing up at me from the stove. I cringe with sadness when I realize she's wearing the red apron with the Golden Gate Bridge on it that Dad bought her on our last visit to San Francisco.

"I'm having cereal," I mumble, as she begins to lecture me on how I need something more filling if I'm gonna be dancing. Ignoring her, I reach for the milk from the refrigerator. *When did she ever care about my love of dancing? It was Dad who cared, not her.*

While I eat my bowl of Apple Jacks, Momma shoots off question after question about the dance studio. I want to tell her it's none of her business, but instead I give her short answers just to shut her up. After that, I go back upstairs to my bedroom and watch music videos until Tyrone finally texts me that he's outside waiting for me.

As I climb into the front seat of his dirty Honda, Tyrone says, "Hey, Zee, are you excited?"

"Yeah, but I'm very nervous."

"That's normal," he says, pulling away from the curb and heading toward the freeway. "It happens to me every quarter with each new class."

"Really?"

"Yeah, but don't worry—it goes away after the first day."

Fifteen minutes later, we exit off the freeway into Al Mar. We drive several blocks until we arrive at Bravo Dance Studio. When Tyrone pulls over to drop me off, I can feel my heart doing somersaults. "I'm going over to Denny's to study," he explains, as I climb out of the car. "I'll pick you up around 11:15."

I can't get the worry out of my head as I head for the entrance. *What if this is a bad idea? I'll probably be the*

only black girl there and what if the girls don't like me?
Taking a deep breath, I open the front door and go inside.
Marivel is standing next to the whiteboard. The second she
sees me, she says, "Perfect timing—follow me to the
back—most of the girls are already here."

Trying my best to calm my wobbly voice, I blurt out,
"What am I supposed to do?"

Marivel smiles, patting me on the shoulder. "Don't
worry, just follow my lead. We always begin with a warm-
up. I know you already met some of the girls, but I'd like
to do a more formal introduction now that you're my assistant."

There are about a dozen girls of different shapes and
sizes on the dance floor talking with each other while they
take off their shoes. As soon as they spot us, two of the girls
come racing up to Marivel. "*Maestra*, can we play
Anville's songs today."

"*Híjole*—I don't have him on my playlist, but maybe
next week," she says. Then, raising her voice slightly, she
asks the girls to form a circle on the floor. Just then, two
more girls dash into the room, hurrying to take off their
shoes so they can join us. Once they're sitting with us,
Marivel asks the little girl next to her to begin the introduc-
tions. "I'm sure you all remember Zakiya. Let's please
begin by telling her your name, your grade and if you've
had other dance classes."

"I'm Quetzali, but everyone calls me Quetzi," says the
tiny girl with the beautiful braids. "I'm in the second grade
and I love to dance. This is my very first dance class."

When Marivel leans over to embrace her, as I suspect-
ed, I realize I'm the only black girl in the room. *This isn't*

the first time, I tell myself as we continue with the intro-ductions. There are two girls who are sisters, but they can't speak any English so Marivel translates for them. Their Spanish is so beautiful and perfect that it makes me think of Carlos.

"They're from El Salvador," the big girl next to me whispers.

Once we're finished going around the circle, it's time for me to introduce myself. Taking a cue from Marivel, I anxiously state, "My name is Zakiya, and my family lives in Laguna. I'm in the 10ᵗʰ grade and I've been taking dance classes since junior high." Pausing for a second, I add, "And I'm super excited to help Marivel." Slightly embar-rassed, I glance down at the dance floor.

"Let's show Zakiya how happy we are that she's my new assistant," Marivel says.

When they all begin to clap, I feel the tension in my neck slowly disappear. *Maybe this wasn't such a bad idea,* I think to myself. *Maybe they will like me.*

Asking everyone to stand, Marivel says, "Let's begin with warm-up." Then she presses the playlist on her iPhone as we all turn to face the mirror that covers the entire wall. I recognize the song by Beyoncé as we all spread out on the dance floor. After she demonstrates the warm-up exercises, Marivel asks me to take the lead while she walks around the room observing each girl. Every now and then, she pauses to pull a girl's arm up higher so that she can stretch her body even more.

After about fifteen minutes of warm-up exercises, we pause to put our shoes back on. Then Marivel orders the girls to form four separate lines so that we can do across the floor exercises. "We'll be practicing chaîné turns now. These are a series of turns in sequence across the floor," she explains, adding, "Let me demonstrate first." The girls watch intently as Marivel sails across the room from the left to the right, then back again several times. Once I've repeated her demonstration, she instructs me to lead the group while she observes each girl. After that, she signals for us to gather at the center of the floor. "Now, we're going to learn a piece of the choreography—this means an actual dance move. We're going to learn pivot turns."

Just like before, Marivel demonstrates the pivot turns several times. Then she has me go to the front to lead the girls while she walks around correcting them. For the next fifteen minutes, we all work on pivot turns, which have always been easy for me. The tall girls seem to do very well, but I notice that the younger students like Quetzi have the hardest time doing them.

We're doing our cool down stretches when the parents begin to arrive. I imagine they're all shocked to see a black girl at the dance studio teaching their kids. Quetzi waves to her dad as Marivel says, "Our time is up, but you all did great. Zakiya, thank you again. We really needed your help."

It makes me happy when several of the girls shout in unison, "Bravo, Zakiya!" Before she races off to put her shoes back on, Quetzi walks up to my side and gives me a hug. Then Laura, the tallest girl in the group tells me, "*Bien hecho, maestra.*" I thank her, using the best Spanish pronunciation I know.

After the girls have left, Marivel and I return to the reception area. Just then, Tyrone texts me that he's here, so I turn to Marivel and say, "I had so much fun, thank you."

Her huge brown eyes glittering, she says, "Are you kidding? I'm the one who needs to thank you—the girls loved you! I do hope you'll return next Saturday."

"Yes, I will," I answer smiling as Marivel gives me the same hug she shared with each of her students before they left the dance studio.

On the drive home with Tyrone, I describe every single detail about my first day of teaching. I'm so excited. "It was so much fun and the girls are so cute, respectful too. They even have a name for me in Spanish—*la asistente.*"

"That's cool," Tyrone says, pausing for a moment. "You know, Zee, Dad would be so proud of you."

My eyes are suddenly misty. "Can we go by the cemetery?" I whisper.

"Sorry, I can't. I have to meet with the Black Student Union. One of the most important African American scholars, Cornel West, is coming to speak and we're meeting with him before his lecture."

Although I'm disappointed, I realize Tyrone is right. Dad would've been so proud of me today, but of him too. We might live in a low-income neighborhood, but we've never had to work in the fields like Quetzi's parents. Dad always used to say that was the hardest work whenever we drove past farms, or saw the workers in the company buses being dropped off in town. Then he'd talk about our ancestors who were brought here as slaves and forced to work like animals in the plantations. Now I understand the poem, "*Edúcate,*" that Mr. Villamil read to us one time in class. It mentioned kids dropping out of school, teen moms, kids involved in gangs. My favorite verses were, "I want to spread my wings / soar high above the skies / get a Ph.D., become a scientist, / teach our children in the barrios." I didn't quite get the message then, but I do now.

TWENTY
Zakiya

On Wednesday I'm coming out of my English class, when I come face to face with Peyton and two of her new friends. Before she can look away from me, I mumble a faint hello. Her friend Piper's eyes widen in astonishment as she continues on past me. When I get to my locker, I wonder what the heck compelled me to do that. I'm supposed to be so done with her as a friend that I haven't even wanted to be near her. Feeling like a stupid jerk, I hurl my books in my locker and head to Performing Arts.

Once we've finished our warm-up, Mrs. Jessup explains that we're going to watch a short video that takes place at the Debbie Reynolds Dance Studio in Los Angeles. When Carly, who thinks she's the best dancer in class, asks who Debbie Reynolds is, Mrs. Jessup explains that she was a famous actor and singer. Before she turns on the video, Mrs. Jessup asks if anyone has ever spent time at a dance studio. Without thinking, I raise my hand. I can feel everyone's eyes on me, including Dalana. Then Mrs. Jessup asks me if I can say a few words about it. Hesitating, I nervously explain that I'm an assistant at Bravo Dance Studio in Al Mar. Mrs. Jessup compliments me as I hear big-ass Jody say, "Show off," from behind me. I'm totally shocked when I hear Dalana's words loud and clear accusing Jody of being jealous.

The second class ends, I hurry and put my shoes back on, looking around for Dalana, but she's already left the gym. I guess I can't blame her. I said some awful things to her the other day. I suppose I really hurt her by bringing her dad into it. *But, what do I care? I don't need anybody anyway.*

During lunch, I'm standing in line at the snack cart when I overhear two girls talking about Becky. The short blond girl asks her friend if she heard what happened to her. When her friend shakes her head no, the blonde girl says, "She's long gone. I guess she cut herself so badly this time that her parents flipped out and sent her away to some treatment place."

"Lucky for her," the other girl says as they both start to laugh.

Scary thoughts begin to swirl in my head as I pay for my drink and hurry across campus to a secluded spot by the bleachers. *What if that had been me instead of Becky? What if Momma had sent me away? I would never want to live anywhere else except here in Laguna. I know Momma can be a bitch, Jerome too, but what would I do without my family, without Tyrone?* I barely nibble on my sandwich unable to think about anything else except Becky.

It isn't until Spanish class that I'm able to stop thinking about Becky. Just as I am about to head through the door, I feel someone tap me on the shoulder. Pausing, I turn around to find Carlos' intense brown eyes staring at me. "Hey, heard you're working at the dance studio in Al Mar."

"How do you know that?" I ask in bewilderment, attempting to stay calm and not have a meltdown in front of his handsome face.

"My dad's *compadre* has a daughter who goes there. She was the one who mentioned you."

"What's her name?"

"She has some weird Mexican name."

"Is it Quetzi?" I ask, my heart pounding wildly.

"Yeah, that's it." He grins as the bell rings and we hurry inside to our seats.

I'm totally surprised to find a substitute teacher standing at the front of the room. While she politely introduces herself as Señora Smith, all I can think about is Carlos. *I wonder what Quetzi said about me. What if she said I was a bad teacher? Or what if Carlos thinks I'm this stupid black girl butting in where I don't belong?*

When Señora Smith asks us to pair up and review the new chapter dialogue, Carlos comes up to me and asks if I want to be his partner. I hesitate for a few seconds, but he cheerfully exclaims, "*¡Ándale, muchacha!*" I can't help but smile, so we find an empty spot at the back of the classroom. After we've read the dialogue and gone over the questions in Spanish, we switch back to English.

"That's cool that you're helping out at Bravo," Carlos says encouragingly. "Quetzi likes you—she said you're really a good teacher."

"She's so sweet," I answer, feeling a sense of relief. "I like her too. But I know they think it's strange, a black girl working there."

"Not really," Carlos says. "There's a lot of black people in Spanish-speaking countries—Puerto Rico, El Salvador, all of Latin America. Besides, who cares what anybody thinks anyway?"

I give him a shy nod. If only I could be that self-assured again. If only I could go back to what I used to be like before Dad died. Just then, Señora Smith orders us back to our seats and I can't help but feel disappointed. "Good luck at Bravo," Carlos tells me as we return to our desks. I'm suddenly feeling light as the clouds in the sky. *Maybe Carlos is starting to like me again.* I can feel my heart beating fast as I imagine him holding my hand.

When I return home from school, I grab a soda from the fridge, then head upstairs to relax before Momma gets home and starts bossing me around. Just as I reach for my cell phone, Jerome cracks the door open. "So I heard you're a cutter now?" he says, a sneer on his face.

"Shut your stupid mouth!" I scream at him, feeling the anger bursting inside. But before I can cuss him out, he slams the door shut and disappears to his room. I jump from my bed and go after him, only he's locked the door. I'm pounding and pounding on his bedroom door when I hear Momma's voice call out for me like she always does the second she walks in the door. I rush down the stairs and walk right up to her as she's taking off her coat.

"You did it, didn't you?" I accuse her in a shrill, angry voice.

"Did what?" Momma asks, her tired eyes searching my face with apprehension.

"You couldn't wait. You had to go and open your big mouth to Jerome?"

Now there are streaks of fear on Momma's face. "Zakiya, calm down—you're hysterical. I didn't tell him nothing."

"Liar! You're always trying to protect Jerome!" I snap, turning back toward the stairway to control my anger. When Momma attempts to follow me, I warn her to stay the hell away. Then I flee to my bedroom, locking the door behind me. My body trembling, I begin to pace around the room in circles until I finally stop and reach for my backpack. I turn it upside down while I frantically search through it, until I find the sharp metal tip of a binder clip. Just as I am about to pierce my wrist, I hear a voice call out to me, "Zakiya, don't do it." I let go of the binder, closing my eyes for a moment. It is then that I turn to gaze at Dad's picture on my bedside, remembering what Ms. Martínez said, that I could call her any day, any time I needed to talk with her. Sitting on the edge of the bed, I take a deep breath as I quickly dial her number on my cell. When Ms. Martínez answers, I whisper, "It's me, Zakiya."

She immediately asks, "Is everything all right?"

"No, it's not," I admit, wiping away the tears sliding down my face. "I wanted to cut myself again."

"Can you tell me what happened?" she gently asks.

In a shaky voice, I describe the whole scene with Jerome and Momma. "I got so mad. I know it was Momma who told Jerome."

I can hear Ms. Martínez inhale. "I can understand how all of this made you feel angry."

"Yeah, it did. Then Jerome has to throw it in my face."

"I'm sure that made you feel even worse."

"Yeah, it did, but Jerome's a little creep."

Ms. Martínez listens to me patiently for the next few minutes while I vent about Jerome. When I've finally calmed down, Ms. Martínez asks, "Would you like me to come over right now?"

"Thanks, Ms. Martínez, but I feel so much better now. It really helps to talk to you about it."

"I'm glad. Now, can you come by tomorrow after school?"

"Yes, I can."

There is a slight pause, then Ms. Martínez asks in a soft voice, "Zakiya, will you be all right until then?"

"Don't worry, Ms. Martínez. I won't do anything stupid."

"Good, but remember, I'm only a phone call away."

After we hang up, I hold Dad's picture against my chest.

TWENTY-ONE
Dr. Martínez

The minute she sat down, Zakiya blurted out the question that was burning inside of her. "Can Momma send me away like they did Becky?" Her eyes were wide with fear. "I heard these girls saying Becky cut herself so badly that her parents sent her away to some treatment center."

"I see." I nodded, waiting for her to reveal more about her friend Becky, only the room filled with silence as her eyes darted around nervously. "Can you tell me more about Becky?"

"There's nothing more to tell," she answered, looking down at her feet.

My voice steady and calm, I explained, "Some parents do choose to send their children away for more intensive treatment, but it generally occurs under specific circumstances when they fear for their child's safety."

Zakiya let out a deep sigh, leaning back in her chair and releasing her pent up anxiety. "I won't let that happen to me, that's for sure."

"Yes, and that's a good thing," I agreed. "Let's talk about yesterday. Can you tell me exactly what happened to get you so upset?"

"It's all Momma's fault," she insisted, sitting up straight. "She didn't have to open her big mouth to Jerome. I got so mad that I wanted to cut myself again, but I called you instead."

"I'm very glad you did that. But please remember what we talked about in the last session with your mother, that it's important for everyone in the family to know what's happening."

There was an awkward moment of silence as she crossed and uncrossed her legs. "Momma denied telling Jerome, but I know she did it. I got so angry that I wanted to hit her, but I didn't. I went to my room instead. That's when I called you."

"Can you describe your feelings when you almost cut yourself?"

"It was like the other time—I was so mad. I felt so angry inside. Like I wanted to bust somebody's face. Then I felt empty and alone inside and that's when I wanted to hurt myself so I could feel better." Pausing for a moment, Zakiya bowed her head, her eyes misty as she went on. "Ms. Martínez, I never used to be like that but ever since Dad died, I get that way." Her voice broke and she reached up to brush away the tears sliding down her face.

"Death is painful," I nodded, handing her a tissue as I thought about Frank. *How often had I replayed the entire scene in my mind, the officer's solemn voice on the telephone that night, the tragedy that changed my life forever?*

"I loved my dad so much—he was the only one who really knew me. Ms. Martínez, you might think I'm crazy, but when I was about to cut, I heard a voice telling me not to do it. At first, I got a little scared, but then I realized it might be my dad. He was always trying to protect me."

"I don't think that's crazy at all," I reassured her, knowing that a day didn't go by that I didn't feel Frank's presence at my side. "No, Zakiya wasn't crazy at all."

"Dad always believed in me, not Momma. All she wants to do is get rid of his things, his clothes, but I won't let her." Her words were defiant like the tears in her stricken eyes. I bit down hard on the inside of my lip until I tasted blood.

"Your mother is also hurting inside," I began. "Death affects the entire family and it takes time for everyone in the family to readjust."

"That's what Father Brown told me," she admitted, her eyes full of fiery streaks, "but that still doesn't give her the right to mouth off about me to Jerome."

"Zakiya, do you think there might be a better way to handle your feelings next time you feel angry?"

A puzzled look appeared on her face. "I don't know, it all happens so fast and I want to lash out. That's when I think about hurting myself."

Measuring my words carefully, I raised my voice slightly. "It's important to be aware of when you're feeling like that, to be mindful of your emotions when this happens."

"But how do I do that?" she asked, sniffling.

"One thing that works is engaging your body by doing something you enjoy."

Zakiya grinned. "I love to dance, but there's no way I could dance when I'm in a rage like that. No way."

"What about listening to music—isn't that an important part of dance?"

Zakiya was pensive for a moment. "Yeah, I guess I could try that. I'm always watching music videos."

"How does music make you feel?"

A huge smile spread across her face. "It makes me forget about everything, it's like when I'm at the dance studio. I really love it. Helping all those girls makes me feel good." The energy in the room had suddenly shifted and I could feel warm vibrations coming from Zakiya. "I'm very glad to hear that. Now here's something to think about—how would you feel if the girls knew you were cutting?"

Zakiya shook her head fiercely. "I wouldn't like that at all. They kind of look up to me. And one day I'd like to be a dance teacher, get my college degree like Ty."

"All the more reason to learn more effective ways to cope with your negative emotions. There's something else I'd like for you to try when you're feeling upset." I reached for the small turquoise journal on my desk. "This is for you."

"It's beautiful," she smiled. "But what's it for?"

I couldn't resist a chuckle. "I know hardly anyone likes to write today, but journaling your thoughts is another excellent way of releasing your negative feelings. Next time you feel upset, I'd like for you to try it. I want you to take out your journal and write down your thoughts, what upset you and why."

"Okay, I'll try it," she agreed, smiling. Then, checking the time on her cell phone, she briskly stated, "I have to go. I told Ty I'd meet him at the corner."

∽ ∽ ∽

I was busy putting some notes in my files when my cell phone rang. It was Sonia inviting me to meet her for dinner at the Thai-Na-Mite. She seemed surprised when I didn't hesitate at all, agreeing to meet her in an hour.

When I arrived, Sonia was already sitting in one of the small booths next to the window. It was a cozy spot since it faced the street and we could *chismear* about the people going by.

"I'm so glad you could come," she greeted me. As usual, she looked as perfect as a magazine cover dressed in one of her trendy professor outfits.

"Me too," I replied, sliding into the booth across from her. "Is Glenn joining us?"

"He can't. He has a Parent/Teacher Conference tonight. *Ni modo*, but sorry I haven't called. We've been having all these protest rallies on campus, you know about the deportations. And since I'm the MEChA advisor, I'm always there to support them."

"Yes, I saw it on the news. It's disgusting."

"By the way, I already ordered."

I had to grin. It was just like Sonia to want to be in charge of everything.

"So, how are you?" she gently pried. "You look great."

"Thanks, so do you," I said, pausing to serve myself some tea. "And if you mean about Frank, I'm better. There isn't a day that goes by that I don't cry for him, but going back to my practice full-time has helped so much."

Sonia reached out to stroke my hand. "I'm so glad—I knew it would. Maya told me you've also been counselling Tyrone's sister."

"What a little *chismosa*," I said teasingly.

"Like mother like *hija*," Sonia admitted, tilting her head back and chuckling.

"You know I can't discuss anything specific about my clients, but ever since I began meeting with Zakiya, I feel better. I know this sounds like shrink talk as Maya would say, but helping Zakiya cope with her father's sudden death is also helping me. I can't explain it, but I feel such a strong connection with both Zakiya and her mother. It's as if their grief is mine and vice versa."

"Sandy, I know exactly how you feel. My Raza students come to me all the time for help, no matter what time of day. They even come to my house. They validate who I am. I see myself in them and it's because of them that I've survived on our conservative campus. So I do understand."

I felt my heart beating faster as I blurted out, "But I still miss Frank so much. I hate going home at night. Frank's presence is in every corner of the house."

"I know," Sonia said, stroking my hand while tears filled my eyes. "Have you heard anything from Frank's family?"

"Yes," I whispered. "I was stunned when Frank's mother called the other night. We had a long talk and she actually apologized for accusing me like she did. She said she knew how much Frank had always loved me and she admitted she was wrong."

"It's about time—that old *vieja*!" Sonia nearly shouted, making me smile.

When the waiter suddenly appeared, I breathed in the delicious smells of Thai food, exclaiming, "I'm starved!" Then I began to fill every inch of my plate with pad thai noodles, chicken curry and rice.

TWENTY-TWO
Dr. Martínez

On Friday afternoon, I'd just walked into the house after an exhausting day when my phone began to ring. Pulling it out of my briefcase, I was surprised to hear Mrs. Cameron's voice: "Dr. Martínez, would it be possible for us to talk today?"

Her words sounded urgent as my gaze drifted to Frank's familiar spot in the living room, his faded yellow armchair. "Of course," I said, looking down at my feet. "Would you like to meet at your apartment?"

"Tyrone gave me your address—if it's all right with you I can come to your house? It's just, well, I don't have much privacy at the apartment. I can be there in fifteen minutes. I told the kids I had to work late."

"Yes, that would be fine," I reassured her.

Hurrying into the bedroom, I thought about the timing of Mrs. Cameron's unexpected visit, receiving a phone call from both Zakiya and her mother the same week. As I changed into my comfortable jeans, I felt a mild rumbling in my stomach, so I went into the kitchen to grab a quick snack before Mrs. Cameron arrived. Biting into a slice of cold leftover pizza, I imagined Frank at the kitchen table late at night sneaking junk food into his *pancita*. Frank could eat anything from frozen burritos to spam sandwiches. Only now everything was different. The kitchen, which had once been one of our favorite spots in the house, now seemed as desolate as my heart. I hated eating alone and I hated being here without Frank.

At the sound of the doorbell, I rushed to open the front door. Mrs. Cameron was dressed in a pair of dark brown slacks and a plain green shirt. There were dark circles under her eyes. "Thank you, Dr. Martínez, for seeing me like this," she explained. "I came straight from work."

"You're very welcome," I replied, inviting her into the living room. Avoiding Frank's armchair, I sat on the opposite end of the couch from her.

"I'm sure Zakiya told you about our fight," she hesitated. "I know you can't say anything, but I've had it. I don't know what to do anymore. She's totally out of control, attacking me. Father Brown said I should pray more, but that's all I've been doing."

My thoughts went back to that day when I'd talked with Father Brown in the church courtyard. It seemed so easy for him to believe that prayer solved everything. But all the prayers in the world could never bring Frank or Mr. Cameron back to us.

"I was afraid she was gonna push me like the last time," she confessed, her voice thick with emotion as she struggled with her words. "I know it's been hard for Zakiya since Jerry died, but she always blames me. She even accused me of telling Jerome about her cutting. She wouldn't let me explain, called me a liar."

"Mrs. Cameron," I began, "the last time the three of us met, you mentioned having a family meeting with Jerome to talk about Zakiya's cutting. Have you done that yet?"

"That's what I was gonna do, but Jerome already knew. I guess he overheard us. But I made him promise he's not gonna say anything to set Zakiya off like that again."

"I think it's imperative that the four of you, including Tyrone, sit down and talk with Zakiya about her self-injury. But, of course, first you and Zakiya need to discuss exactly what she wants everyone to know. I can't emphasize enough that when parents try to keep it a secret from the rest of the family, it always backfires on them."

Mrs. Cameron shook her head, pursing her lips. "I still don't understand how this can be happening to my daughter—she was always the quiet one, the sweetest child. Now I'm so afraid she'll kill herself—I search her room whenever I can. I make sure I know exactly where she is at all times."

"Policing a teen only makes things worse. They're experts at hiding things from their parents. If Zakiya wants to hurt herself, she'll find a way."

Releasing a sigh of frustration, she promptly admitted, "I don't know what to do anymore."

"I know how difficult this must be for you, but one of the first steps is to learn to talk differently to Zakiya. Parents often adopt a critical attitude with their teens. Instead of listening to them, they end up being judgmental. Every teenager needs to know that they're being heard and not judged, especially those who are self-injuring or suffering from any kind of emotional distress."

"But how do I do that?" she demanded in a tired, thin voice.

"It takes a great deal of effort and patience. But with time, you can learn new ways to communicate."

"I tried asking her about the dance studio, but she was obnoxious and rude. All she does is scream at me, attack me. If only Jerry were here."

If anyone knew how she felt it was me. There wasn't a single day that I didn't find myself wishing Frank were still here, that I could hear his voice one more time, that I would hear his car in the driveway and find him standing there with a bouquet of flowers. Now here we both were, two lonely widows connected by grief.

Wiping away a tear, Mrs. Cameron raised her head, looking intently at me. "I never realized how much easier it was when Jerry was here. It's hard working full-time now to make ends meet. I feel stressed out, on edge all the time."

I reached out to pat her hand. "Mrs. Cameron, things will get better. I'm working closely with Zakiya to help identify the sudden emotions she's been feeling since Mr. Cameron died. We're making progress. Zakiya's a lot like you, strong, resilient, and I promise you I won't give up on her."

A faint glimmer of hope appeared in her weary eyes as she blinked back tears. "I also want you to know that you're not alone. There are many resources out there to help families like yours. Have you ever considered taking a parenting class?"

She pursed her lips, shaking her head forcefully. "Of course not," she replied. "Jerry was always very private. He always insisted we take care of our own family problems. That's why we had family meetings since the kids were little."

After years of working in marginalized communities, I completely understood her resistance to seeking outside help. The need to rely solely on the power and strength of the family was also very common in Chicano and Latino communities. "Mrs. Cameron," I began, choosing my words carefully. "I think it's great to work things out as a family unit. However, there are times when parents can't do it alone and they may need outside help. I'm familiar with a local organization called Parent Project that offers free parenting classes for families whose children are undergoing emotional issues."

Mrs. Cameron drew in a quick breath, glancing at her watch. "Time to get home," she explained, rising from the couch. "I have to make some dinner before Tyrone gets home from the university."

At the door, I paused to hand her the small blue handbook on top of the bookshelf. "I want you to have this—I think this might help. It has some very useful information on how to parent a teen girl."

"Thank you, Dr. Martínez," she smiled, tucking it in her purse. I feel better already and I promise to read this. I'll do anything to help Zakiya."

As I closed the door behind her, my eyes rested on Frank's armchair until I found myself moving slowly across the room. Pausing for second, I reached down to caress the worn armrest before I let my body sink into it. It was here that Frank had buried his grief that desolate Sunday morning when we'd learned about Kobe Bryant's tragic death. He'd spent the entire day in his old armchair glued to the television mourning with Laker Nation. Closing my eyes, I leaned back and breathed in the scent of Frank, allowing it to permeate every cell in my body. I thought of Zakiya then, her desperate need to cling to her father's things. In that moment, I knew that I would never rid myself of Frank's armchair.

TWENTY-THREE
Zakiya

As the bus drives through the familiar city streets to school, I try not to think about my birthday, but the decorations on the streetlamps remind me that Christmas is a few weeks away. I always wanted to be that magical number, sixteen, but today all I can think about is that it will soon be my first Christmas without Dad. He loved this holiday the best. It was the only time he would go shopping with Momma to pick out a special gift for each of us. And Momma would get so mad at him because he couldn't wait to find out what his presents were, so on the sneak, he'd open his gifts when he was alone. Then he'd rewrap them again, acting like he'd never seen them before.

A while later, I'm standing at my locker, when Peyton comes up behind me. "Hey, Zakiya. I know it's your birthday today," she says handing me a card. "Alan said to tell you happy birthday too." Before I can thank her, she disappears down the noisy hallway.

I wait to open the card until I'm in English class and Mrs. Harrison is discussing one of Shakespeare's more boring sonnets. It's a beautiful card, very colorful and powerful with seven Kwanzaa dancers on the front. On the inside, it reads *Happy Kwanzaa* and both Peyton and Alan have signed it. I remember the day Peyton asked me about Kwanzaa. When I explained how it symbolizcd pride in our African heritage, she thought that was so cool, saying her grandparents were very proud of their Irish background. Carefully placing it inside my binder, I wonder if this is Peyton's way of letting me know she's still my friend despite the pissy way I've treated her.

In Performing Arts, we've just finished our warm-up when Dalana appears at my side. "Hey, happy birthday," she says. I'm even more shocked when she cautiously asks, "How's the dance studio going?"

"Cool," I answer as Mrs. Jessup orders us to line up to practice movement across the floor.

"See you," Dalana says, moving back to the other side of the gym next to her friend Joanie.

After that, I'm filled with remorse. I have a hard time focusing on the new dance step Mrs. Jessup is introducing. Weeks have passed since Dalana and I had that terrible fight. Maybe it's time to let it go just like with Peyton. Maybe it's like Tyrone said, Dalana was only trying to protect me, that he would've done the same thing for one of his friends.

By the time I get to Spanish class, I'm feeling as if this isn't going to be such an awful birthday after all. Even though Carlos is absent today, I don't let it get to me since I'm not as distracted. I'm able to concentrate better on today's lesson. All I know is I'm more determined than ever to learn Spanish so that one day I can be bilingual like Marivel and communicate with the students at Bravo.

After school, I'm surprised to find Tyrone's Honda parked by the bus stop. "Hop in, birthday girl," he says, rolling his window back up while I hop into the front seat. "What are you doing here?" I blurt out.

Tyrone flashes me a huge smile as he makes his way carefully out of the busy parking lot. "I wanted to surprise you on your big day," he confesses, his voice husky and cheerful just like Dad's. For a moment, I want to scoot closer to him, lean my head on his shoulder and lose myself in all his love and protection. But instead I gaze out the window.

When we arrive back at the apartment, I'm surprised to see Momma's black purse on the end table. The next thing I know, she comes walking out of the kitchen. There is a half-smile on her face and she looks relaxed. "Happy birthday, Zakiya," she says, taking a step toward me as if she wants to embrace me. Hesitating, she turns to Tyrone to ask, "Son, did you pick up what I needed from the store?"

"Yes, ma'am," Tyrone replies, handing her a small bag that I hadn't noticed before.

Before I can disappear upstairs to my room, Momma cheerfully states, "No dishes tonight. Jerome's doing them since it's your special day."

Lying on my bed with my books, I can't believe the words that just came out of Momma's mouth. All she ever does is treat Jerome like a spoiled baby. She's definitely not feeling well, that must be why she's home early. I've just finished an hour of Algebra homework when Tyrone opens the door and announces that it's time to eat. When I explain that I'm not finished, Tyrone's voice softens. "Come on,

Zee," he pleads. "Momma came home early so she could make you a special birthday dinner."

"All right," I begrudgingly agree. I'm completely surprised when I walk into the kitchen to find a large Happy Birthday sign taped on the wall next to the table, which is covered with the red Christmas tablecloth. There are also two yellow and green balloons taped to the chair where I usually sit.

"It's your favorite," Momma says, pointing to the delicious-smelling baked chicken on the counter. It's obvious Momma's trying her hardest to please me.

"Thanks," I mumble, wishing it were Dad seated at the head of the table instead of Tyrone. Every year on my birthday, Dad would repeat the entire story of the day I was born, chuckling at how fast I came out compared to Tyrone. And he always ended by saying, "Zee baby, you were our best Christmas present!" Swallowing hard, I am forcing back tears just as Jerome rushes up to the kitchen table. Momma gives him a warning look while she places the platter of chicken and the salad on the table.

"Hey, big sis, happy birthday," Jerome says in his usual whiny voice. "Wish I were sixteen."

I force out a smile, it's so weird that he actually cares and he's not out bumming with his juvenile friends.

"Momma, this is delicious," Tyrone compliments her after taking several bites of a drumstick. "What do you think, Zee?" he asks, looking straight at me.

I can feel Momma's eyes on me. "Yeah, it's super delicious," I reluctantly admit. When her face lights up big time, I can't help but remember how much Dad loved Momma's cooking.

As soon as we're done eating, Momma orders Jerome to help her gather up the dinner plates. I'm about to rise from the table when Tyrone says, "Wait up, Zee." Moments later, he orders me to close my eyes. When I'm finally allowed to open them, I find a round birthday cake with thick creamy chocolate icing at the center of the table. "I made it myself," Momma proudly admits while Tyrone helps Jerome place sixteen red and blue candles on the cake.

After they sing "Happy Birthday" to me, I make a wish and blow out the candles with Tyrone and Jerome's help. Then Momma promptly announces, "Now it's time for presents." Handing me a red envelope, she adds, "This is from Aunt Martha."

I eagerly open the card, which has a huge number "16" on the front. Inside of it, Aunt Martha has placed a fifty-dollar bill. "Man, I need some cash," Jerome teases, attempting to snatch it away from me. Momma quickly reaches out to slap him on the hand, reminding him it's not his birthday.

Next, Tyrone hands me a mid-sized box wrapped in shiny green paper that I recognize from the campus book-store. When I open it, I find a beige T-shirt with the words *Black Student Union*, written across the front in big bold letters.

"I love it," I exclaim, holding it up to my shoulders. "Thanks, Ty."

"Maybe one day you'll also join BSU," he grins.

"I will for sure," I nod, reaching out to give him a hug.

When Tyrone tells me he hopes it's the right size, pissy Jerome says, "Yeah, Zakiya, you *are* kind of big."

"Shut up," I snap back, while Momma gives him another scolding look. I knew his fake niceness was too good to be true. But not even *he* can ruin my mood. Turning back to Tyrone, I say, "It's perfect—I'm gonna wear it tomorrow to show it off."

I'm completely bewildered when Momma hands me a small red box with a matching bow. "This is from me and Jerome," she says, an apprehensive look on her face. I let out a short gasp when I open it to find a beautiful heart-shaped locket on a sterling silver chain. "Go on, look inside," Momma gently tells me. My heart is racing and my fingers are trembling as I open it to find a picture of Dad when he was young.

"It's a picture of your dad when he was your age," she says, wiping away a tear from the corner of her eye. "I thought you would like it."

"Oh, Momma, thank you," I whisper, holding it up so that both Tyrone and Jerome can see Dad's picture.

"No wonder I'm so handsome," Jerome brags as Tyrone helps me put it on. Pressing it tightly against my chest, I feel an intense wave of joy as if Dad were here at my side and we were all together just like before. In that moment, I realize that Momma really *does* care about me. "This is the best present ever!" I tell her, and soon we are both hugging and crying.

TWENTY-FOUR
Zakiya

On Saturday morning, I'm surprised to find Father Brown at the dance studio. He's standing next to Marivel and I can tell they're having a serious conversation because their heads are bent and their voices are hushed. It's the first time I've seen Father Brown dressed in jeans. He almost looks like a normal person if it weren't for the white clerical collar under his blue shirt.

"Well, hello, Zakiya," he greets me. "How's your mother doing?"

"Better," I answer him, while Marivel moves closer to embrace me.

"I was waiting for you so we could get started," she says. "Only, it's a small group today." Her words are tight and out of sync like an untuned guitar.

"Then I better get out of here so you can get started," Father Brown says, and then he looks directly at me. "Marivel tells me you're doing awesome and the girls really like you."

"Thank you, Father Brown," I reply, noticing how the smile on his face is fading as he turns back to Marivel.

"I'll call you the minute I have any news about the girls."

The serious tone of his voice tells me that something isn't quite right, so the second the door closes behind him, I ask Marivel, "Is something wrong?"

Shaking her head in disgust, she explains, "It's about Martita and Dulce, the two sisters from El Salvador. I guess *La Migra*, you know, ICE, picked them up and deported their parents. Father Brown is talking with a Human Rights Organization to see if we can find out where the girls were taken."

"What?! You think they were taken?"

"We think they took them to one of those detention camps on the border somewhere."

"Can they do that?" I ask, horrified. "They're only little girls."

"*La Migra* can do anything they want," Marivel emphasizes, angry tears seeping out of her green eyes. "Come on, the girls are waiting. There's a lot of anxiety in the air today, so let's begin with a small *plática.*"

"What's that?" I ask, wondering if it's a type of body movement or dance stop.

"Sorry," she apologizes. "It means a short talk to clear the air."

As soon as we walk in the room, Quetzali races up to give me a hug. Then Marivel instructs everyone to sit in a circle on the dance floor. "We're doing something different today," she explains. "I want each of you to close your eyes and keep them closed until you've thought of something good you did for someone during the week. The room grows silent and after about a minute the girls are ready.

Marivel points to Yolanda, who is sitting across from her and asks her to go first. Blushing, Yolanda says, "*Híjole*, I guess I helped my mom peel the *papas* for dinner last night."

While Marivel compliments her, Quetzali starts waving both hands wildly in the air, blurting out, "I gave the baby his bottle when Amá was busy cooking!" Several chuckles fill the air as we continue going around the circle. When it's finally my turn, I hesitate, wondering if I have anything positive to share. Then I remember how last week I helped old Mrs. García carry her groceries upstairs to her apartment. This inspires María, the tallest girl in the class, to offer, "My *abuelita* lives with us and I help her with heavy stuff every single day." By the time everyone has shared their good deed, the energy in the room has shifted from dark and gloomy to bright morning sunlight.

After that, we begin our warm-up to the hip-hop sounds of Anville. First, we do several sequences of pointing and flexing to warm up our ankles. Next, we review the pivot turns from last week. Then Marivel introduces the new step or the knee turns, which I've practiced before in my dance classes. She demonstrates the exercise, making it look super easy going from one leg to the next. As usual, Marivel has me move to the front of the group while she walks around observing. I can tell the girls are feeling more comfortable with me now because they constantly call me to their side for help. This makes me feel even more proud of being Marivel's assistant.

It isn't until the end of class when we're putting our shoes back on, that I overhear two of the teen girls talking about *La Migra*. Marina comments on how her parents are having to be extra vigilant, making sure their green cards or US passports are with them at all times. "I hate *La Migra,*" Alicia exclaims. "My mom won't let us out of her sight, she's so afraid."

Dad always talked to us about how black people were treated in this country. He would often talk about Malcolm X, his fearlessness and courage in standing up against white supremacy and police brutality. And one time when I visited Aunt Marilyn, she took me to the Black Panther Exhibit at the Oakland Museum. Every photograph, every newspaper, captured the police brutality and racism that Dad talked about. I was able to experience Dad's passion for how Malcolm X influenced not only the Black Panthers, but the entire Civil Rights Movement.

Driving back to Laguna with Tyrone, I tell him about Father Brown and Marivel's conversation. "Yeah, it's terrible," he agrees with a scowl on his face. "We've already had several student protests on campus about the forced separation of parents and their children and the targeting of anyone who looks Mexican."

"I'm so glad about the protests," I tell him, feeling even more proud of Dad for teaching us to fight for social justice. He was always quoting Malcolm X and Dr. Martin Luther King Jr. and saying how they didn't just care about black people, but about anyone who was oppressed.

After Tyrone drops me off, I find Momma in the living room reading a book. When she sees me, she immediately tucks the book under her as if she doesn't want me to see it. But as soon as she stands up, I'm able to scan the title. It says something about how to communicate with teen girls. *Is she crazy or what?*

Momma comes back. She asks, "How was the dance studio today?"

"It was both good and bad," I sigh, but before I turn toward the stairway, she invites me to sit down and tell her all about it. I hesitate, but the caring look on her face pulls me toward her.

"Tell me the good first," she begins as I sit next to her on the couch.

"It was so much fun. Father Brown was there."

Momma's lips part in a half-smile. "That man's like your daddy, always on the move." Pausing for a moment, her voice suddenly turns serious. "Your daddy would be so proud of you—he always said you were the best dancer."

"He wasn't so bad himself," I grin, as the light in her eyes begins to dim. I wonder if she's imagining all the times Dad would scoop her up in his big arms and they'd prance around the apartment. All of a sudden, the words fly out of my mouth, "I want to be a dance teacher one day like Marivel."

"Your daddy would like that," she nods, her voice almost a whisper. "Just like he always told you kids, you can be or do anything you want."

"Thanks, Momma," I reply, wondering if Momma's heartache is as big as mine.

"Now tell me about the not so good," Momma insists, attempting to sound cheerful.

When I tell her all about the two little girls from El Salvador who were taken away from their parents, Momma's face grows somber. Her voice quivering, she confesses, "I'd die if someone took you and your brothers away from me. Children are the most precious gift in the world. We carry you in our womb, you're part of our life line."

There are tears in Momma's eyes as she scoots closer to give me a hug, only this time, I don't push her away. I'm reminded of Martita and Dulce and how awful they must feel being separated from their mothers.

Later that evening, I'm staring at the beautiful card Peyton gave me and before I can stop myself, I'm calling her on my cell. When Peyton's voice comes on, I say, "It's me, Zakiya."

Despite the fact that I haven't called her in weeks, Peyton's words are light and cheerful as if nothing ever happened between us. "Hey, Zee, how's it going?" she asks. I can hear the excitement in her voice.

"I wanted to thank you for the birthday card—it was so cool."

"I picked it out just for you," she proudly reveals. "When I saw it at the Hallmark store, I knew you'd like it."

I'm feeling all choked up inside by an overwhelming flow of emotions. After a very long minute, Peyton breaks the heavy silence, "Zee, are you still there?"

I can feel myself breathing faster. Sucking in a deep breath, I spill out my confession, "I'm sorry for being such a bitch, for the way I've been acting. Do you think we can be friends again?"

"I would like that a lot," Peyton immediately replies. "Maybe we can go to the mall and hang out next week. I know Alan will drop us off."

"Cool," I tell her, feeling an intense joy penetrate through my entire body just like when I'm at the dance studio with Marivel and the girls.

TWENTY-FIVE
Dr. Martínez

"You're looking very pretty today," I complimented Zakiya, as she took a seat across from me. She was wearing a bright yellow sweater with a matching skirt that made her face glisten like moonlight. I could feel the energy radiating from her body.

"Things are way better, terrific actually." She smiled, leaning back on the chair in a comfortable position.

"Great—can you tell me about it?"

Uncrossing her long legs, she sat up straight. "Momma's acting human again. She did the nicest thing. Last week was my birthday, so she made me a cake and even gave me this." Placing her right hand on the locket around her neck, she held it up for me to see. "It has a picture of my dad in it when he was real young."

"That's quite a special gift," I said. "It's beautiful."

Her face beaming, she went on. "Then at school, Peyton gave me this really cool card, so I broke down and called her one night. We're friends again—we hung out at the mall yesterday."

"That's great news. Friends are extremely important in our lives." I thought of Sonia then and how we'd been through so much together. I knew deep in my heart that I couldn't have made it through Frank's death without her friendship.

Zakiya's face fell for a moment. "I wish I could be friends with Dalana again, but I was so mean with her."

"You've not mentioned Dalana before."

"Dalana's in my Performing Arts class—she's the one whose dad's in prison, but I called her some real bad names." Pausing for a moment, she went on, "But she's been acting friendlier—she actually stood up for me in class the other day. I want to make up with her, but I'm not sure how to do it. "

"Sometimes people need time to think things through. Just be yourself and give it time like you did with Peyton."

"Yeah, I'll try," she nodded. "But I was so mean to her."

I drew in a quick breath, my throat tightening. It was time to talk about her cutting. "Zakiya, have you had any more urges like the other night to hurt yourself again?"

Reaching up for a strand of her long curly hair, she began to twirl it nervously. Hesitating for a second, she slumped down in her chair, her voice sounding distant and far away. "I thought about it, but I didn't do it."

"Can you tell me about it?"

Zakiya straightened out her shoulders, her dark eyes peering into mine. "It's about the dance studio," she began, her voice rising sharply. "I got really upset because there are these two little sisters from El Salvador who were taken away by ICE. Their parents were deported too, but no one knows where they took the little girls to. It made me so angry when I found out."

"I can understand why this upset you. It's very disturbing and it's been happening more and more lately."

Lowering her voice, she leaned forward. "I don't understand how this can happen to those little girls, they're so sweet and innocent."

"I know how awful you must be feeling about this," I reassured her.

"Yeah, I got so angry, sad too, that's why I felt like cutting. But it helped talking about it with Tyrone. Momma was real understanding too."

"It's good that you talked with them about your feelings. And it sounds like you and your mother are communicating better."

"Yeah, she listens now instead of bitching, sorry, like she always used to."

She paused for a few seconds, her face brightening. "When I feel like cutting, I do what you suggested. I try to focus my mind on something else that feels good like music or I pick up the journal you gave me and I write about what I'm feeling. This really helps me get my anger out."

"That's wonderful that you're remembering to be mindful, to be aware of your emotions."

"Yes," she eagerly nodded. "And it really helps being at Bravo Dance Studio. I really love helping Marivel and the girls."

"Can you tell me how that makes you feel?"

"It makes me feel so good inside, so proud like I never want to let the girls down. They sort of look up to me now like they do with Marivel."

"You're absolutely right about that. You've become an important role model for them."

"Do you really think so?"

"Of course, I do," I reassured her, noticing the sparkle in her eyes. "Now, can we talk about your relationship with Jerome?"

Zakiya frowned. "He's still a little punk, but he was nicer on my birthday. Momma talked with him and we're gonna have a family meeting next week."

"I'm glad to hear that, but do remember to make sure you and your mother come to an agreement beforehand about what you will and won't discuss."

"That's exactly what I told Momma—she agreed with me right away."

"That's great. Zakiya, I'm very proud of you. I know it's hard work, but you've already made so much progress."

"Thanks, Ms. Martínez," she said, her voice lowering for a second. "But it's still not the same without Dad."

"Yes, I know," I agreed, thinking about my own life and how it had drastically changed without Frank.

When Zakiya's phone abruptly interrupted us, she quickly scanned her text message, then jumped to her feet, exclaiming, "It's Tyrone, gotta go!" Before sprinting out of my office, she reached out to give me an unexpected hug. "See you next week, Ms. Martínez," she said. "And Ty was right—you're the best!"

Later, when I arrived back at the house, instead of hurrying off to my bedroom to change, I took several steps into the living room, pausing to gaze around at the faded beige walls that Frank had always teased he was going to paint purple and gold like his Laker flag. Smiling, my eyes were drawn to the small fireplace where we would sit on cold winter evenings and sip our favorite Chilean wine. "Frank, this is our home," I whispered, tears springing to my eyes. It was here that Frank and I had nurtured our love, survived the miscarriage of our first and second child, laughed, cried together.

Feeling a lightness in my heart that I hadn't felt in a very long time, I went back to the entryway and reached for my briefcase. Taking out my wallet, I searched for Father Brown's card. My pulse racing, I reached for my cell phone and dialed the number on the card. The moment I heard Father Brown's deep voice, I quietly said, "Father Brown, it's Sandra—Dr. Martínez. I was wondering if we could meet and talk sometime soon."

TWENTY-SIX
Zakiya

It's Friday morning and the halls are buzzing with excitement since it's the last day before Christmas break. Everyone's hyped up, cracking jokes, talking about how they're gonna sleep until noon everyday, not open a single book. Even the nerdy guys seem anxious for vacation. Me, I'm gonna kick back too, but what I'll miss the most is going to Bravo Dance Studio on Saturdays. Marivel said they're closed until January but that she expects me back after the holidays.

As soon as I walk into the gym, I spot Dalana near the back talking with Joanie. I'm suddenly compelled to apologize, to tell her I was the one who acted like a bitch, not her. Remembering Ms. Martínez's advice about being myself, I hurry over to their side before Mrs. Jessup can start the warm-up. "Can I talk to you for a second?" I ask Dalana, ignoring Joanie's cold stare as she joins another friend at the front of the gym.

"What's up?" Dalana cautiously asks, raising her perfectly shaped eyebrows.

Shifting my weight nervously, I stammer, "I'm sorry for the way I've been acting. I know you were only trying to help—do you think we can be friends again?"

My cheeks are burning hot, so I lower my head, staring at my feet. I can feel a queasiness in my stomach and I'm unsure of what to do next when Dalana gently places her hand on my arm.

"I'm sorry too, Zee," she begins in a soft but firm voice. "I shouldn't have butted in."

"It's okay—I would've done the same thing."

"I've really missed you," Dalana admits, "especially on your birthday."

"Me, too," I tell her, my heart jumping wildly.

Just then, Mrs. Jessup orders us to begin warming up. We move back to the center of the gym, only this time we pick a spot next to each other. I'm suddenly feeling strong as an eagle soaring high in the sky with Dalana at my side.

At lunchtime, I meet Peyton at the snack bar and we walk over to sit on a bench near the main quad. When I tell her about making up with Dalana, she raises her fist high up in the air, cheering so loudly that several heads turn to stare at us. "Maybe the three of us can meet at the mall this weekend," Peyton suggests once she's calmed down.

"That would be super cool," I agree, adding, "or as my Spanish teacher would say, "*¡Excelente!*"

Peyton's small lips part in a grin at my imitation of Mr. Villamil. Then a serious expression appears on her small face. "I'm really happy you're back, Zee. Just in time too, we're having a volleyball meeting tomorrow—want to come with me?"

I give her a scrutinizing look. "Do you think Coach would mind? I haven't been participating at all."

"Are you kidding? Coach asks about you all the time. Besides, he needs his star player back on our team!"

We burst into more giggles and one of the guys on the grass hollers at us to shut up, but we ignore him. Then, while Peyton gives me more details about the volleyball meeting to discuss next season, I picture myself starring in one of those Marvel films wearing a tight, sexy outfit. I'm holding a shield in one hand and my spear in the other one. I'm about to save the world just like Wonder Woman!

After that, I'm off to Algebra class feeling so happy inside, wondering if I'll be able to talk with Carlos next period. When Mr. B asks me a question about the boring algebraic formula he's just finished explaining, I stare helplessly at his bony face. I'm relieved when Melvin, the Math genius, rescues me with the answer, then rushes victoriously to hit the magic gong on Mr. B's desk.

The second I walk into Spanish class, I glance toward Carlos' seat, only it's empty. Feeling disappointed, I take my seat, but just as the tardy bell rings, Carlos dashes into the classroom. While he takes his seat, he looks in my direction and gives me a huge smile. My heart fluttering, I smile back at him. Afterward, I'm unable to concentrate on Mr. Villamil's review of the stem-changing verbs. When he instructs us to pair up to go over the exercises, Carlos quickly moves toward my side of the room.

"*Vámonos*, Zakiya!" he greets me. "Let's sit over there next to Frida."

Feeling excited and hopeful, I follow him to the back where Mr. Villamil has decorated a corner of the room with a bright Mexican rug and a framed poster of Frida with her monkeys. We take turns completing the exercises, but as soon as Mr. Villamil steps out of the room, Carlos switches to English. "I heard about what happened to the two little girls at the dance studio."

"I can't believe it—it's so disgusting," I tell him, keeping an eye out for Mr. Villamil.

"Yeah, there's more *Migra* raids now than ever before," Carlos nods.

"I'm even thinking of going back to MEChA because of that. I dropped out for a while, but I want to see if there's anything we can do to help those two innocent little girls."

"That's cool," he nods. "Count me in, one of my friends is in MEChA and they do a lot to support social issues. I've thought about joining it myself."

In that moment, Mr. Villamil suddenly reappears and begins to circulate around the room. We shift our focus back to the Spanish exercises, but before we continue, Carlos looks at me with his gorgeous Mexican face. "Want to go see a movie with me this Saturday?"

In absolute shock, I whisper yes as Mr. Villamil orders everyone back to their seats. While Mr. Villamil spends the rest of the period drilling us with the new verbs, all I can think about is my first date with Carlos. It's all I've ever wanted and it's finally coming true!

After school, I'm feeling like this is the best day of my life, so I decide to avoid the bus home and go by the cemetery so I can visit with Dad. I'm walking near Discount Foods when an idea suddenly pops into my head. Hesitating for a few seconds, I cross the street and make my way through the parking lot all the way to the entrance. I hurry inside to where the fresh flowers are at and pick out a bouquet of bright yellow daisies. Then I walk slowly toward the back to the Seafood counter where I pause to breathe in the familiar smells that remind me of Dad. When the tall husky man wearing the white overcoat asks if I need any help, I whisper, "No, thank you, it's just that, my dad used to work here." Before he can ask me another question, I spin around and disappear down the nearest aisle. I'm heading back toward the front of the store, when I spot Maureen, Dad's old friend and coworker. She's standing next to the canned food section.

"Zakiya," she gasps. "What a nice surprise. How are you and the family doing?"

"Much better," I explain. "I just came in to buy some flowers for Dad."

"Those are beautiful," she says, sighing tenderness in her eyes. "We still miss Jerry a lot. Everyone asks for him all the time."

I can feel my eyes getting misty, so I quickly say, "I have to pay for these now. I need to go by the cemetery."

Before I can take a single step forward, Maureen snatches the bouquet of daisies out of my hand, demanding that I follow her to an empty register where she promptly rings up the flowers. "No charge," she insists, handing them back to me. "And please don't forget to tell your daddy hello for me and that we all still miss him."

At the cemetery, I hurry through the entrance and go straight toward the back until I arrive at Dad's gravestone. I bend down to carefully place the flowers in the empty gray vase. "These are for you, Daddy," I say, sitting down on the cool grass. "I got them at Discount Foods. Maureen says hello—she wouldn't let me pay for them. She said everyone still misses you." I pause for a moment to wipe away the tears. "But I wanted you to know that I'm feeling way better now, Dad. I'm working at Bravo Dance Studio and it makes me so happy. You know how much I love to dance and the girls are so cute." Reaching for my locket, I hold it up. "Momma gave this to me for my birthday. It has your picture in it—see, you're right here with me all the time. And Momma's trying to be nicer. I know she misses you too." I reach out to caress his picture on the gravestone, whispering, "I love you so much, Daddy. And I want you to be so proud of me, just like you are of Tyrone." Tears filling my eyes again, I rise to my feet. "But I better go now before Momma gets home. I'll always love you, Daddy. I'll be back soon."

GLOSSARY

¡Ándale, muchacha!—Come on, girl!

anoche—last night.

Ballet Folklórico—traditional Mexican dances that emphasize local folk culture with ballet characteristics.

Bien hecho, maestra—Well done, teacher.

chismear—to gossip.

chismosa—[female]; gossipy person.

comadre(s)—midwife; colloquially used to refer to a close family friend, a relative by mutual consent that may not be of blood.

cumbias—a kind of dance music of Colombian origin, similar to salsa, which is popular in Mexico and throughout Latin America.

Edúcate—Get an education.

¡Excelente!—Excellent!

Está muy contento—He's feeling good.

Hija—daughter.

Híjole—Wow! My goodness! Oh my gosh!

jalapeños—a very hot, small green chile of Mexican origin.

la asistente—the assistant.

La Migra—short for Inmigración or "Immigration" as it refers to the Border Patrol; for Mexicans and Chicanos the use of this name has invoked fear since it refers to an institution that has historically harassed and abused Mexicans crossing the border dating back to Anglo-American colonization of the Southwest in the 19th century.

MEChA—Movimiento Estudiantil Chicano de Aztlán; a student organization founded during the Chicano/a Civil Rights Struggle of the 1960s.

Ni modo—Oh, well.

pancita—small stomach.

Panzón—fatso; a big-bellied person.

papas—potatoes.

Raza—race, lineage, family. La Raza is a concept that includes all Latinos regardless of nationality.

¿Te gusta bailar?—Do you like to dance?

¡Vámonos!—Let's go!

vieja—old lady.

Also in the Roosevelt High School Series

Ankiza

Forgiving Moses

Juanita Fights the School Board

Maya's Divided World

Also in the Roosevelt High School Series

Rina's Family Secret

Rudy's Memory Walk

Teen Angel

Tommy Stands Alone

Tommy Stands Tall

Tyrone's Betrayal

Gloria L. Velásquez created the Roosevelt High School Series "so that young adults of different ethnic backgrounds would find themselves visible instead of invisible." When she was growing up, there weren't any books with characters with whom she could relate, characters that looked or talked like Maya, Juanita or Ankiza. The Roosevelt High School Series [RHS] is her way of promoting cultural diversity as well as providing a forum for young people to discuss serious issues that impact their lives. She often will refer to the RHS Series as my "Rainbow Series" since she modeled it after Jesse Jackson's concept of the rainbow coalition. Furthermore, the impact of books such as *Tommy Stands Alone* have made their way into Banned book lists.

Velásquez has received numerous honors for her writing and achievements, such as being featured for Hispanic Heritage Month on KTLA, Channel 5, Los Angeles, an inclusion in *Who's Who Among Hispanic Americans, Something About the Author* and *Contemporary Authors*. In 1989, Velásquez became the first Chicana to be inducted into the University of Northern Colorado's Hall of Fame. The 2003 anthology, *Latina and Latino Voices in Literature for Teenagers* and *Children*, devotes a chapter to Velásquez's life and development as a writer. Velásquez is also featured in the 2006 PBS Documentary, *La Raza de Colorado*. In 2007, she was also included in the award-winning anthology *A-Z Latino Writers and Journalists*. In 2004, Velásquez was featured in "100 History Making Ethnic Women" by Sherry York (Linworth Publishing). Stanford University recently honored her with "The Gloria Velásquez Papers," archiving her life as a writer and humanitarian.